HOLLOW POINT
A ZOMBIE NOVEL

DEDICATION

I would like to dedicate this book to my beautiful wife, Jessica, and my wonderful sister, Keely. You two are the most important thing in my life.

NOW AVAILABLE AND COMING SOON
FROM
OPEN CASKET PRESS

RATS
BIGFOOT TALES
ZOMBIE BUFFET
CREATURE FEATURE
DEAD CHRISTMAS
WARRIORS OF THE APOCALYPSE: BOOK 1

HOLLOW POINT
A ZOMBIE NOVEL

MARK CHRISTOPHER

HOLLOW POINTS: A ZOMBIE NOVEL

1

The American soldier knew he was in trouble the moment he opened his eyes. His first conscience thought was that he couldn't move. He tried moving his arms slowly at first and immediately stopped as the coarse rope that was tied around his hands began to burn into his wrists. He began to kick with his legs, but realized they were also immobilized.

He arched his sore neck down and noticed black, plastic zip-ties firmly secured around his ankles. His boots had been removed and his bare, pale feet were now a dusty brown from the dirt floor.

Where the hell am I? he wondered while slowly looked around the dark room.

His head ached horribly with each back and forth glance he made. He could feel the source of the pain pulsing from the back of his head.

The back of my head? he thought.

Then he remembered.

2

"Just another day in this shit box!" the soldier yelled to the other as the Humvee sped forward.

The other soldier nodded his head in agreement; his eyes were fixed on the dirt road ahead.

"Hey, Tanner, you all right up there?" the soldier behind the wheel called to the gunner above.

"Doing just fine, Tex. Ready to get the fuck home and get some food in me."

"We're almost there, Cajun. Just a few more miles to go," Tex said with a smile to the silent Cajun, whose eyes never left the side of the barren desert road.

Then Cajun saw it; saw something in the faint distance. A group of kids, no more than ten years old, were running from behind a cluster of large rocks. They were jumping and dancing, smiling and waving as the soldiers all turned to look at them.

"What the hell are they so happy about?" Tanner asked from above.

They all heard the shriek coming from the opposite side of where the kids had gathered. It was a decoy, and a most clever one.

"Shit!" was all Tanner could yell before the Humvee was struck with a rocket-propelled grenade.

The side of the Humvee erupted in a mass of twisted metal and sparks. The three soldiers were all flung in various directions and the shredded vehicle came to a dead rest. The one called Cajun tried to lift his face up from the sand. His mouth was filled with grit and blood. Then quickly the world began to spin. White lights danced before his eyes until the white faded to black. He collapsed into the sand and was still.

3

He knew where he was now and the fear gripped him as his heart slammed wildly into his chest and an icy chill ran down his spine. The sounds of footsteps drawing closer caused the hairs on the back of his neck to prickle. He could hear muffled Arabic coming from the room next to him, and the conversation was getting louder with each passing second.

Suddenly, the door to the room swung open and in strode two men. They were similar in features; both tan from the desert sun and each had long, black beards covering most of their faces.

"Fuck both of you! I'm not saying shit!" the soldier screamed, startling the two men at the ferocity of the sudden outburst.

A thunderous fist rocked the soldier's jaw, causing him to feel dizzy for a moment.

"Let's go, American," the first man to enter the room said.

The other withdrew a large knife and reached behind the soldier, cutting the ropes restraining his arms. He brought the knife swiftly to the soldier's neck.

"Do not be stupid, American," he hissed into the soldier's ear.

The men each grabbed an arm and dragged the soldier out of the room. He wobbled down the sandy path with his captors until they approached a metal door. The one who had whispered into his ear stepped forward and pounded on the door, causing the soldier's head to ring. The door opened quickly and they were ushered in by a man wearing a black ski mask over his face. The soldier was led to a single wooden chair and forced down. His arms were twisted behind the back of the chair and restrained with plastic zip-ties. A thick, copper-like smell filled his nostrils. He also felt a wetness seeping into the bottom of his desert camouflage pants. He was startled when an unexpected voice boomed from in front of him.

"How do you Americans say it? Ah yes, It's show time!"

4

A bright light shone in front of him and he squinted as the sudden light burned his sensitive eyes. Then the entire room filled with light as bare light bulbs hanging from wire began to flicker on. When his eyes became acclimated to the light, he fully understood how grave his predicament was.

The light that had blinded him initially belonged to a video camera set atop a tripod. He noticed the camera was horribly outdated. The Iraq flag hung to his left and the Afghanistan flag to the right, both on badly corroded metal flag poles.

Behind him stood three men all wearing black ski masks. The one in the middle held a brown-stained machete and the other two, one on each side, held Kalashnikovs.

The soldier looked down at the ground and located the source of the metallic smell. What he saw almost made him gasp in horror.

Dark, burgundy blood was mixed with the dirt around his chair. He was certain he'd identified the wetness he felt in the seat of his pants. He turned to his right, not wanting to look down, but instead saw something much worse.

Two pairs of legs were stretched out from behind a pallet of sandbags. They were wearing the same desert camouflage pants as him.

"You motherfuckers! I'll kill all of you!" he screamed as he fought against the plastic ties. He could hear the man behind him let out a snort of laughter.

It was pointless, that he knew, but he would be damned if he gave them the satisfaction of knowing he was afraid.

The man near the camera nodded his head toward the one holding the machete.

The soldier felt his head yanked back violently as the machete man palmed his head like a basketball. A filthy, wet sock was crammed into his mouth and duct tape was secured around his head.

He did his best to breathe through his nose and keep his tongue away from the sock, but it was futile.

The foul liquid ran down his throat, causing him to gag as his taste buds were flooded with a horrible sensation of spoiled vinegar and moldy cheese.

Please don't throw up, he begged himself and mercifully his body listened.

"Now we begin," the man near the camera said. He flipped a switch on the ancient camcorder and stepped in front.

5

The soldier noticed the man in front of the camera was different from the others. He had long black hair that appeared clean and a smooth-shaven face. A long scar traced its way from his right eye down to the corner of his mouth. He appeared to have no problem showing his face.

He had no idea what the man was shouting into the camera, the Arabic flowing from his mouth like a waterfall. However, he knew what it was probably about. *Blah blah blah...leave our land...blah blah blah...kill the infidels...blah blah blah...praise be to Allah!* is what he imagined. Then the man switched to English.

"We have killed two of your heathen soldiers and we will kill this one as well. We will take the head of a new soldier every day until you Americans leave our homeland! We have a pen of prisoners waiting to be beheaded!"

Bullshit, he thought.

Scarface then paused for a moment, as if he was contemplating something. He broke his concentration and walked to the camera, flipping it off. He turned and walked in front of the soldier and lowered his face; locking his eyes to the prisoner's.

"Tell us the location of your unit and we will spare you. Do what I say and you will be a free man."

The soldier did his best to block out the rotten onion smell permeating his nostrils from the man's skin. This new stench was too much and the soldier knew he had to do something soon or he would vomit, possibly choking himself to death.

He nodded his head.

"Allah be praised!" Scarface proclaimed as he ran back to the camera and switched it on.

"You see, Americans! We will drag what we need from the mouths of your whipped boys! Remove his gag!" he ordered.

Machete ripped the tape off and with it pieces of hair from the soldier's head. He didn't care. He gasped at the sweet air as the sock was removed, then spat onto the ground until his mouth was dry.

"Go on, tell us! Tell the world!" Scarface yelled, laughing like a lunatic.

"Behind...the...road..." he choked.

"What?" Scarface asked.

"Behind...the road..." he whispered again, trailing off at the end of the sentence.

Scarface walked over to him again and stopped a few inches from his face. He dropped to one knee and locked his eyes again onto his prisoner's.

"One more time," Scarface requested as a sick smile crossed his face.

He responded by spitting into Scarface's eye. "I said fuck you, you camel-humping piece of shit!" he screamed and laughed.

Scarface wiped the spit out of his eye. His brown face was now marooned with rage and humiliation.

The three men behind the soldier began to move but Scarface raised a hand, making them stop. Scarface walked over to the pallet where the bodies laid and returned with a large piece of wood.

The soldier's crazed smile faded when he knew that wood was coming for him. With a savage scream, Scarface swung the wood hard, snapping the soldier's right shin like a twig.

He wanted to scream but found the pain paralyzed him. His breath rushed out of him like a balloon being popped and he felt immediately nauseous.

Scarface walked around him slowly, eyed his left leg, and swung like a lumberjack. The left shin splintered like a dry chicken bone. The pain was so excruciating that he knew he would be passing out soon. His vision was already starting to fade.

"Kill him!" Scarface ordered, his face still red with anger.

I didn't give them the satisfaction, the soldier thought as he waited for the end.

Machete stepped forward and raised his weapon high. Screaming praise to Allah, he brought the weapon down.

The soldier closed his eyes, expecting to feel the blade slice into his skull, when Machete suddenly stopped his blow, his head exploding. Like fireworks in a chain reaction, the heads of the two soldiers carrying the Kalashnikovs erupted in a shower of red mist.

The soldier opened his eyes and saw Scarface turning around, his mouth agape in confusion. Then his head evaporated like the others.

The sounds of bombs erupted in the background as bits of rock showered down on the barely conscious soldier, a dust cloud rolling through the room. Through blurry eyes, he saw his saviors emerge from the cloud. The Army Rangers had come.

One of them stepped forward and placed a hand on his shoulder.

"You're gonna be all right, Sergeant!" the Ranger yelled over the bombs. The Ranger turned and signaled another man over. "Both his legs are broken! Cut him loose and help me get him out of here!"

The bombs continued to explode in the background as everything faded to black. Though the soldier couldn't see, he could still hear the dull thuds.

The thuds kept getting louder and strangely hollow. Hollow like a fist hitting a door.

6

Eight years later.

Former Army Ranger and current sheriff, John Boudreaux, opened his eyes and looked around his dirty house as the pounding on his front door roused him, rescuing him from reliving a past nightmare.

He wiped his sweaty face with his hands and felt the prickly stubble on his face. His eyes were a dull blue cloud set against a blood-shot backdrop. They had been a crystal blue once, but years of drinking and pain pill abuse had distorted them. He sat up on the couch and felt the crack of his sore joints and the aching of his bones. His head throbbed like it always did when he woke up.

On the coffee table in front of him was a half empty bottle of Miner Dan's whiskey. It was one of the cheapest brands the grocery store carried, and the way he drank whiskey he couldn't afford the good stuff. A dirty glass shining with whiskey residue sat next to the bottle. He had at least used a glass this time. The sun cast its fiery rays into his living room from the large window behind the couch that he'd been slumbering on and painted a grim picture. Magazines and beer cans were strewn about the small living room and a half-eaten sandwich had wedged itself behind an old chair.

A picture of him, his ex-wife, and daughter when she was only eight, was on display on a shelf containing a few books—none he'd actually bothered to read. They all wore smiles in the picture and John wore his deputy police officer uniform with pride. It reminded him of happier times. Those were times when he didn't wake up screaming, thinking his legs were being broken by terrorists; times when the pain from the hours of rehabilitation on his legs caused him to cry. It didn't take long for depression to follow. He would go to the gun range for hours some days, shooting until the paper targets were reduced to shreds just to take his mind off his life. But it never lasted for long, and when the last round was fired, the depression came upon him again like a swollen rain cloud. It wasn't long before he came home one day to a note saying his wife had left him and had taken their daughter, and divorce papers would be arriving soon.

The banging on the front door resumed. He turned his head and squinted at it, annoyed his one tranquil moment was being taken away.

Go away, he thought, then yelled, "What do you want?" from the couch, not trying to hide the aggravation in his voice.

"Sheriff? It's me, Mike!" the voice called back. "I need to talk to you, John."

John sighed and lifted himself slowly off the couch. His shins burned with each step toward the door. They always burned when he woke up.

7

John gripped the dirty brass handle and opened the front door. It was unlocked, of course. The sun attacked his eyes violently, causing him to go temporarily blind. He could feel the heat of the sun burning down on his face and he raised his hand to shield the painful rays.

Deputy Mike O'Neal took a step forward and blocked the sun. At twenty-four years old, Mike was the youngest deputy for the

Cypress Pass police force. He had the typical look of a big, country boy. His large frame had been perfect for high school football and college as well. He'd put on some weight after college and now tipped the scales at a little over two hundred and eighty pounds. He stood at six and a half feet tall; his size certainly was an advantage when it came to dealing with trouble makers.

Those that knew him, however, had learned he was a gentle giant, always having a goofy smile plastered across his large face. He was wearing one of those smiles when John opened the door.

"What's up, Mike?" John sighed; it was way too early for Mike's good mood.

"Old lady Reynolds called the station earlier, Sheriff. She said her husband's missing."

John left the doorway and went back to his couch. He motioned for Mike to follow him inside. Mike entered slowly and closed the door behind him, the rays of the sun burning furiously against the door. Sweat began to run down the back of Mike's neck as he entered the house.

A single box fan was positioned in the corner of the living room and it circulated the warm, swamp air around the room. John sat down on the couch, grabbed the whiskey bottle, and poured himself a shot. He drank it down quickly. The warm burn always soothed his sore throat.

Better than coffee, he thought.

He offered the bottle to Mike who put a hand up in refusal.

"She called in saying that he went out last night for a lottery ticket and a carton of smokes but never came back. I think she's more pissed about the cigarettes not coming home than her husband," Mike said with a chuckle.

John picked up his pack of cigarettes from the brown end table next to the couch. He searched his pockets, and not finding what he wanted, placed his hand between the couch cushions, then started lifting magazines on the coffee table.

"Where's my damned lighter?" he grumbled.

"Uh, Sheriff..." Mike said as he pointed his finger. John followed it and saw his blue, ninety-nine cent, plastic lighter atop the small television. Mike grabbed it and handed it to John, who lit the cigarette and took a deep drag. The cancerous smoke filled his lungs. John stood up and looked at Mike, who appeared to be waiting on a response about the Reynolds' situation.

"Just give me a second to wake up, Mike," he muttered as he staggered to the bathroom. His shins burned the entire walk there.

8

John flushed the toilet and walked to the dirty sink. After filling his hands with cold water and splashing it across his face, he looked at himself in the mirror and sighed. The face staring back did not belong to a thirty-five year old. He rubbed his face again and confirmed he needed to shave, but at least the stubble hid the scars on his chin. The vision of a brown right fist colliding with his face popped into his head. He pulled on the mirror and it sprang forward, revealing a medicine cabinet. He removed a bottle of Vicodin, shook two pills in his hand, and swallowed them.

Mike left the trash-strewn living room and entered the kitchen. The counters were bare with the exception of empty beer bottles and fast food wrappers. No dishes were in the sink, because John rarely used them. Mike walked over to the refrigerator and peered at the crudely cut newspaper clippings and pictures hanging on the door. A shopping list was stuck to the fridge by a magnet. It read, *whiskey, beer, cigarettes*. Below the list was a colorful picture drawn by the hand of a child. Two squiggly stick people were holding hands and smiling. One was tall and the other was short with blond hair. They were standing under a smiling sun in a field of purple and gold flowers. The picture made him smile.

John entered the kitchen with the whiskey bottle in his hand. He grabbed the top from the counter and screwed it on tight. He looked better now that he'd shaven and washed up a bit, but he still felt tired and sore. He walked over to the refrigerator and pulled the door open. Mike stepped aside and rested an arm against the counter.

"All right, Mike, tell me what's so important you had to come by on my one day off."

"William Reynolds…" Mike said, waiting for John to finish the sentence.

John didn't finish the sentence. Instead he removed a beer and an egg from the refrigerator.

"William Reynolds is missing," Mike finished.

"Oh yeah, that's right. Last night?" John asked as he grabbed a glass from a cabinet.

"Yes. He went out and never came back."

John popped open the beer, poured it into the glass, then cracked the egg and added it. Mike watched the yolk slowly sink to the bottom of the gold liquid.

"Some people just do that. Hell, he probably had a few beers and fell asleep in his car somewhere. He's been known to do that," John said as he raised the glass, trying not to look at the picture his daughter had drawn for him.

"You aren't really going to drink tha…" Mike began to say. Before he could finish, John had swallowed the beer and egg. A nauseous look washed across Mike's face. John noticed this and gave Mike a big smile followed shortly by a loud belch.

"That's disgusting. I've never seen anyone do that, and I've seen some crazy shit in college," Mike said.

John stared at his empty glass and debated on having another. He decided against it and placed the glass in the sink.

"Since it was last night it's a little too early to file a report. I'll just go down there a little later. Odds are he'll be home by then," John said. He removed his pack of cigarettes from his jeans and popped one out, then lit it and took a few puffs before putting it out. He was trying his best to quit and felt that taking a few drags at a time were better than smoking a whole one. Of course in doing this he smoked double the amount he normally went through in a day.

"You know those are still bad for you, right? It doesn't matter that you only take a few drags and then put them out," Mike said.

"Anything else you need to tell me," John asked, growing more annoyed with each passing second. He knew there had to be a better reason for Mike to come to his home. It certainly wasn't because some old drunk was missing.

"Oh yeah, the mayor wants to have a meeting with you. He said he'd come by the station around eleven."

John glanced at the clock on the wall to see it was 8:53 a.m.

"So much for a day off," he growled.

Mike shrugged his shoulders in a *what-do-you-want-me-to-do?* expression.

9

John left the kitchen, made a quick turn down the hall, and entered his bedroom. He opened his closet, reached in, and removed a dark navy police shirt; the crest of Cypress Pass was stitched to the left shoulder, the American flag was on the right.

Iraq flag on the left; Afghanistan on the right, he thought. He buttoned up the shirt and tucked it into the wrinkled pair of jeans he'd slept in, then removed a pair of socks from the drawer and put them on his feet. He slipped his feet into a pair of black boots and snapped on his utility belt. His .40 was on the dresser; he picked up the gun and holstered it. He found his wallet on the floor and placed it in his back pocket. Fully dressed, John turned off the bedroom light and exited the room, making his way back to the kitchen.

"You wearing jeans, boss?" Mike asked.

"It's casual Friday," John quipped, noticing that Mike was in his standard uniform.

"It's Wednesday," Mike commented.

"Whatever."

"Me and Kelly are goin' fishing this evening if you wanna go. The white perch are supposed to be on the move."

"Sounds good, but I think I may have a date."

Mike looked shock. "With who? Jack Daniels?" He laughed at his joke.

"You know Jack is out of my league," John joked back. He removed his keys from the top of the refrigerator and started to make his way for the front door. Mike wasn't budging without an answer.

"Samantha, from the diner," John finally said.

"Oh really?" Mike smiled as he followed John out of the house. "So you're actually going to talk to a woman again? It's only been what, four years?"

"Three and a half. And you're driving," John said as he locked the door behind him.

10

The two officers drove down the winding highway leading toward downtown Cypress Pass. The highway ran parallel and curved with the swamp that bordered most of the town. The stretch was how Cypress Pass had gotten its name, as the swamp was littered with cypress trees of all sizes, their boney knees sticking out of the murky water. On the other side of the highway were houses and fields. Most of the homes were of the mobile variety but a few old, ranch style homes were mixed in. Only a few homes were located bordering the swamp, and they were further down the highway, away from downtown. The squad car zipped down the highway which was always light of traffic. A white egret flew in front of the car and perched on a cypress knee.

John reclined in the passenger seat while Mike drove. He reached out and fiddled with the radio, but all the stations were playing static.

"It's been like that all day," Mike said.

John clicked it off and sat back in the seat, biting on his thumb-nail. It was a nervous habit. He looked out of the window and stared into the sprawling swamp.

"Did you ever think you'd come back here?" John asked suddenly, catching Mike off guard.

"What do you mean?"

"I mean, look at you. You were the hometown hero, the football star who went on to college and played."

"What's your point?" Mike asked. His trademark smile had faded.

"Just…" John trailed off. "I don't know." He turned to look at Mike. "I mean, we both got out of here. We'd made something of ourselves, and then what? We got dragged back here." He looked back out the window. He really had no clue why he'd started this conversation.

"Blowing my knee out my senior year kind of ended my football career and getting a worthless major ensured I'd be back. That and Kelly was here," Mike said. "What about you, John? You didn't have to come back. You chose to."

"I came back for my daughter and a wife that I thought still loved me. I took this job to stay with them but it turned out she liked it better when I was off playing war. I can't even see my daughter without a court-appointed babysitter. I'd rather not see her at all if I have to have a stranger watch me while I play with my kid."

"Well, why stay here then? Why not move away, start over?"

"I wish I could go back to the Middle East. Don't get me wrong, Mike, this is my hometown. I love these people...this job."

"I think you're depressed, John," Mike said as his smile returned.

John cracked a smile. "I'm not depressed."

"You drink a lot."

John rolled his eyes and laid his head back. "Don't start with that shit."

"Look, I'm sorry," Mike said. "I'm just glad you're going on a date. Meeting someone new will be good for you."

"I know. That's what I'm trying with Samantha."

Mike glanced at John. "I hope it works out for you."

11

A large, wooden sign ahead proclaimed their arrival to Historic Downtown Cypress Pass. John always shook his head when he drove past the sign. The mayor had ordered it to be constructed to try and drum up a little tourism for the quaint town. John wasn't sure what the history of Cypress Pass was and doubted it was interesting enough to have a sign proclaiming it. Regardless, not many families wanted to spend their free time in a mosquito-infested swamp town.

As they crossed over into downtown, the swamp was cut off. The main road was littered with small businesses. A small store selling art and antiques stood next to another store selling music and books, which was nestled next to a small grocery store.

Duplessis' Diner was next to the grocery store and directly across the street was the police station. A volunteer fire department consisting of one truck was next to the police station. A small medical clinic was further down the road. Inside, the doctor operated an illegal dental clinic, but with a dentist more than twenty miles away, the people of Cypress Pass overlooked this. The main hospital was twenty miles away in the town of Bayou Boeuf.

Mike parked the squad car in front of the station and the two cops exited the vehicle. Mike began to walk to the station entrance, but John held back. He was glancing at the diner across the street.

"Hey, Mike, I'll be right back. I'm gonna grab a cup of coffee."

"We have coffee in the station," Mike replied but John was already jogging across the street. Mike grinned and headed into the station, knowing exactly why John wanted to go to the diner.

12

John entered the diner and he was immediately greeted by the smells of bacon, syrup, and coffee. He looked both ways once he entered, trying to spot one particular waitress.

"Mornin', Sheriff. Getcha some breakfast? Biscuits just came out of the oven," Simone Duplessis said.

At sixty-six, Simone still felt half her age. As the owner of Duplessis Diner—she'd been for twenty-five years—she still made her biscuits from scratch and never missed a day of work. Her warm, grandmotherly personality was always a crowd pleaser and she moved her plump frame around the counter with amazing balance for a woman her age. She was holding a full pot of jet-black coffee.

"No thanks, Simone. Just coffee, please."

Simone grabbed a Styrofoam cup from behind the counter and filled it with the steaming coffee, then handed the cup to John.

He turned toward the cigarette machine and placed his money inside. His selection hit the bottom with a soft thud. He removed them from the machine and placed them in his pocket.

"Hey, Simone, is Samantha coming in today?"

"She should be in around noon."

John's spirits brightened and he took a sip of his coffee.

"You know, maybe I'll get a biscuit to go."

A few minutes later, John exited the diner and made his way back to the station. His mouth was full of hot, buttery biscuit. He'd made the right choice in getting one.

13

John placed the coffee on his desk and sat down in the torn, leather chair. He could feel the seat flatten under his weight.

His desk was relatively bare, only holding a cup for pens and a metal bin for police reports. Various papers cluttered the rest of his workspace. Behind him on the wall was a frame holding the numerous medals he had received from the Army. His police academy certificate was framed as well and hung next to a document proclaiming him as the sheriff. Two metal chairs faced his desk, in the rare event he had to entertain anyone.

A stuffed nutria set atop a piece of wood was in the corner. He wasn't sure where that had even come from. John glanced at an unfinished report from the night before involving some teen pissing on the side of the bookstore. Had it have been the Historic Downtown Cypress Pass sign, John would have thrown the report away. He grabbed a pen and began finalizing the report when a knock on his door caused him to look up.

"Come in," he said, and the door opened with a creek.

Diane Miles poked in her head. She'd been the secretary of the police station for forty years now. Her husband had been Sheriff for thirty-eight of those years until a heart attack ended his life four years ago. With John's longevity in the department and military experience, he was the most qualified to take the title of Sheriff. Diane knew her husband would have been proud. At seventy-one, Diane was a little absent minded, but still got the job done.

"Johnny, the mayor is here to see you," Diane said as she ran a hand through her thin, white hair.

"Thanks, Diane, send him…"

Before John could finish his sentence, Mayor Philip Dunlop rushed past Diane and entered his office.

14

Philip Dunlop had been the mayor of Cypress Pass going on fifteen years. He first took office at the young age of thirty-two and had won unopposed every year since. It wasn't that he was a great mayor; he was just a great bullshitter.

When the time for elections came, he always ran the slogan: *If it ain't broke, don't fix it*, and the townspeople agreed with this sentiment.

Born and raised in the Deep South, Philip was a true good ol' boy. He was always dressed in a seersucker suit and a fedora hat, which he wore to hide his thinning brown hair.

He stood a little over six feet tall and a gut was starting to protrude over the pants of his suit. He hid his eyes behind cheap sunglasses, even at night, and spoke in a thick, southern accent that sounded more like Foghorn Leghorn.

John thought he kind of looked like him as well.

"Sheriff, there's someone I'd like you to meet," Dunlop announced as he strode into the office.

John heard, *I say, I say, boy,* and tried not to laugh. His brief self-amusement fled from his mind when he saw the other man step into his office behind the mayor.

The man's gray hair was neatly cut short and his face was clean-shaven. His visage was the same hardened features that only surfaced during years of war.

His eyes were like blue ice on fire. He was dressed in the uniform of a high ranking Army official. John studied his name tag and various colored ribbons and medals that adorned his outfit. An eagle insignia perched on both of the man shoulders signified him as a colonel.

He walked with perfect posture and confidence.

"Morning Mayor," John said as he reached his hand out.

Dunlop grabbed it and pumped his arm up and down enthusiastically. John could feel his headache starting to return. He turned and addressed the officer. "Colonel," he offered his hand, and the colonel gripped it like a vise.

"Please sit down," John said. "Can I get anyone some coffee?"

"No thank you, son, our visit will be brief," Dunlop replied.

"Well then, what can I do for ya'll," John asked as he sat back in his chair. The leather pad let out a whoosh of air as his body weight came down on it.

"John, this is Colonel Jacob Dillon. He's with the Army's 1st Battalion, 249th Infantry Regiment, is that right?" he asked as he turned to the colonel for confirmation.

The colonel nodded his head in agreement.

"And this is Sheriff John Boudreaux. He used to be one of you guys," the mayor told the colonel.

"Oh really? Where at?" Colonel Dillon asked in a deep voice that sounded like a throat full of gravel.

"1st Battalion, 75th rangers," John replied.

"Really? That's great," Dillon said with a smile.

Yeah, real fucking great. Let me show you the scars on my legs and my empty house, John thought to himself. His head was raging and he felt the need to scream at this man but held it in check.

John sensed that something wasn't right. Very rarely had the mayor ever spoken to him except to tell him to arrest whoever was responsible for vandalizing his tourism signs. Now he walked into his office and brought a colonel with him.

"So what brings you to our little town, Colonel? Did you see one of the mayor's signs?" John asked, trying to rush the meeting along.

"As procured through Mayor Dunlop, my unit will be coming here to conduct some training."

"What do you mean by 'coming here'?"

"As I'm sure you've seen on TV, hostilities are starting to shape up once again in the Balkans. I'll say this to you and please keep it between us, but Yugoslavia and Albania are back to fucking with each other again. Intelligence has suggested the possible threat of a nuclear device being used in this conflict by a third country, possibly China due to their close ties to Albania. My Special Forces will need a place to perform some survival training and I think the swamp surrounding your small town will be the perfect place."

John sat back in his chair and stared at him. The colonel shot him a winning smile.

"I just wanted to make you aware of the situation personally, Sheriff," Dillon said. "I don't want your police force or the towns-people being spooked by gunfire or helicopters flying overhead."

John smiled and leaned forward. "What kind of training are we talking about here exactly?"

"Just the basics: survival, POW exercises, and some other minor drills. Nothing too serious. You'll be notified before we use live rounds so that you may alert the public and prevent a panic."

"So you need to train in a swamp to survive in the Balkans? Pardon me, Colonel, but that's bullshit."

"Now calm down, John," Dunlop said, breaking his silence.

The mayor leaned forward in the small chair he was spilling out of. He was eager to hear John's explanation. Colonel Dillon was sitting back with one leg crossed, unfazed.

"Look, Mayor, I've been there," John began, his eyes fixed on the mayor's. "Hell, I've been one of them. I know what it's like to be stuck in a small town with a bunch of your buddies. These Army guys are going to get liquored up and cause trouble when they realize there isn't a damn thing to do around here and I'm already short staffed as it is. There's no way we could handle the trouble."

John paused and turned to Colonel Dillon. "And why the hell do you need mountain survival training here in the swamps?" he asked again, noting that his previous question was ignored.

"The survival training is all the same, Sheriff. The terrain doesn't matter. I just need someplace secluded. Trust me, my boys will be training so hard that all they'll want to do is sleep each night. Plus, no one's allowed to leave the camp, short of an emergency. And we have our own security force to deal with any troublemakers."

"I still don't like this," John said, his eyes creased.

"All right, that's it then," Mayor Dunlop said as he jumped to his feet, his face beet red from aggravation. "I didn't come here to ask your permission, John, merely to inform you and to let you meet Colonel Dillon."

"This is bullshit," John said and stood up as well. Dunlop was really starting to work his last nerve.

Mayor Dunlop turned and looked at the colonel. "Can you please excuse us, sir?"

Dillon stood up, his metal chair sliding a few inches backwards. "No problem. It was an honor meeting a former ranger. See you around, Sheriff."

John nodded his head and the colonel exited the room, closing the door quietly. The two men stood in silence as the sound of Dillon's polished boots faded down the hallway.

"They're nothing but trouble, Mayor. Soon we'll have a bunch of drunken soldiers running around and fighting and just making a mess of things," John whispered through clenched teeth.

Dunlop didn't say anything. He knew starting a shouting match with John would turn ugly fast and get them nowhere. He took a deep breath and reached into the pocket of his coat.

His hand produced a single white envelope. He held the envelope out to John, who hesitated at first, but then grabbed it. John felt a familiar thickness to it. He tossed the envelope on his desk.

"Everything's taken care of. There won't be any trouble, I can promise that. The Army is paying us a lot of money to use the swamp. *A lot.* We need this money, John. The entire town does. We'll be able to do so much good for the people with it, and the soldiers will only be in the swamp. They'll be gone before you know they were even here. Let's just play ball, John, for the good of the town."

John sat back down and gave an, *I give up* motion with his hands. He picked up a pen and began scribbling notes onto a blank piece of paper. The mayor fixed his hat and opened the door to leave.

"Please close my door," John said.

"Sure thing, son," Dunlop said and looked back, "You're doing what's good for the town, remember that."

The mayor left and closed the door.

John waited a full three minutes before he reached for the envelope and opened it.

15

John peered inside the envelope and felt his heart begin to race as the dozens of Benjamin Franklins stared back at him. He laid the money on the desk in neat piles and counted. After he finished, he counted again, convinced he'd counted wrong but he hadn't.

In front of him was ten thousand dollars—cash. A little less than a quarter of his yearly salary lay on his desk. He removed eight thousand dollars and placed it back in the envelope. He would give that to the staff as a bonus once the Army had left town. He figured they would need it more than him.

He reached down to his left and opened a large drawer at the bottom of his desk. Moving back a stack of file folders, he retrieved a metal flask. Unscrewing the cap, he took a long swallow of the amber whiskey. The burning sensation made him feel better. He screwed the cap back on and placed it back in its secret hiding spot.

So much for a day off, he thought.

He remembered he wanted to check on the Reynolds' situation before it got too late in the day. He stood up and exited his office to let Mike know he would need a ride back home.

16

Mike was sitting at his desk, on the phone. Unlike John's office, Mike's gave a window into the kind of person he was. A large redfish was stuffed and mounted above the doorway. Behind him, the wall was littered with pictures of him playing football in high school and college, him graduating the academy, and of him and Kelly. His desk was neat and all his papers were placed in a multi-layer tray in the top left corner.

"Yeah, I know we need a new one," he said as the sound of his wife filled his ears.

John walked into the office.

"Hey, Mike, I need you to..." John trailed off when he saw Mike on the phone. He paused at the door and excused himself, waiting patiently outside the office.

"Okay, honey, lemme go. I'll pass by and check it out. Love you too. Bye," he said and hung up the phone.

"Check out what?" John asked as he walked into the office.

"Kelly wants me to go see a couch at the furniture store. We need a new one, but it's not like we can afford one anyway."

"Can you run me back to my place before you go? I'm going to go check on Mrs. Reynolds."

"Sure, boss, no problem. You want me to go with you?"

"Nah. I'm just gonna ask her a few questions and hopefully scold her husband when I get there."

"All right just give me a few seconds. I gotta take a piss."

Mike quickly walked to the bathroom and John turned and went back to his office. He reached into the drawer and removed a thousand dollars. He tucked it into his pocket, said goodbye to Diane, who waved while talking on the phone, and walked out of the police station to wait for Mike.

17

John was leaning against the patrol car, smoking a cigarette, when he noticed a certain waitress walking toward the diner.

Wearing a white blouse and black pants, she reached the door and opened it while securing her apron around her waist.

He could feel his heart begin to race again.

Guess it's put up or shut up time, he thought as he took a final drag of his cigarette. He dropped it on the ground, stepped on it, and crossed the street to the diner.

He took a deep breath before pushing the diner door open and stepping inside. The smell of grilled burgers came to him, causing his mouth to salivate. The acidic smell of tomatoes also hung in the air, and a glance at the chalk-written specials announced the soup of the day was tomato basil. Samantha Worthing was behind the counter, wiping the syrup spills off the laminated menus.

Samantha was your typical pretty girl stuck in a small town. Her long brown hair was neatly tied in a ponytail and her body was toned and athletic from her morning jog. At twenty-eight years old, she'd stayed behind in Cypress Pass to take care of her ailing grandmother, who had raised her when her parents died in a tragic car accident.

Her other friends went to college or just left to escape the trap that was the small town, but not Samantha. She worked as a permanent substitute teacher in Bayou Bouef, but when school got out each summer, she always went back to work at the diner. She was content here. Things were simple, and unbeknownst to John, she'd noticed him, too.

"Hey, Sheriff, you want your regular table today?" she asked with a smile.

John shook his head. "No, Sam, just some coffee to go please." He returned the smile and was sure she blushed a little.

"Sure thing," she replied, then poured him a cup of hot coffee and handed it to him.

"Thank you," he said and remained at the counter. He started to say something but the words were stuck in his throat. He thought about turning and walking out, but knew Mike would be asking him for details about the date and then giving him another lecture if he failed to go on one.

You'd think this would get easier with age, he thought, feeling like a kid in elementary school who was asking out a girl for the first time. He looked up and she smiled at him. He smiled back and then decided to go for it. "Hey, Sam, do you work tonight?" He was trying his best to quell the nervousness in his voice.

"I'm off around five. Why?"

"Oh…well, I was wondering if you wanted to do something tonight."

It really doesn't get easier with age.

"Yeah, that'd be great! What did you have in mind?"

He wasn't ready for that. He'd been so nervous about asking her out that he hadn't thought of a thing for them do. In a small town, it was pretty hard to think of something. They could take the twenty mile drive to town, but he didn't want to do that. However, he didn't think she would go for shooting cans while drinking.

Actually, he thought, *that sounds like something fun to do later. Oh shit, she's still waiting! Answer her!*

"Mike and Kelly are going fishing tonight. Mike said something about white perch or something."

"That sounds like fun! I haven't been fishing in ages. And then maybe you can cook me dinner with what we catch," she said.

"I can sure as hell try. But I'm not promising anything." A big smile ran across his face. He felt good inside, almost warm. He was enjoying the feeling.

"Pick me up at my place around six-thirty?"

"You got it," he said, and with a wave, he left the diner.

Samantha watched him walk down the steps of the diner and felt her heart was about to explode. She was breathing heavily and could feel the surge of adrenaline rushing through her body, causing her to shake with a mixture of nervousness and excitement. She glanced around the diner and hoped none of the patrons had noticed her childish exchanges with John.

"Samantha! Order's up!" yelled a voice behind her.

She turned and retrieved a plate containing a hamburger and another with a country fried steak.

Back to reality, she thought with a sigh.

18

The squad car pulled up to John's house and he climbed out. He closed the car door and immediately wished he was back in the air conditioned vehicle. The swamp air was muggy and hot and he could already feel his brow getting damp within seconds. He walked around to Mike's window and motioned with his hand for him to roll it down. Mike pressed the button and the window slid down.

"The offer for fishing still stands," Mike said.

"Yeah, I think I might take you up on it. Is it okay if I bring Samantha?"

Mike's face lit up. "Absolutely! The more the merrier!"

"One more thing," John said as he dug into his pocket. He removed the wadded bills and slapped them in Mike's hand.

Mike, for once, was at a loss for words. He looked at the large pile of green bills and tried to stammer a reply.

"Buy the couch, Mike, compliments of the U.S. Government."

There were too many questions running through Mike's head. Finally he was able to get a word out. "How…"

"I'll tell you 'bout it later," John said as he walked to his front door.

Mike drove away with his head dizzy from excitement. He was trying not to swerve as he counted the money over and over again. Within seconds, his hand reached for his cell phone so he could tell Kelly the amazing news.

John waited for Mike to turn the corner and then he walked up the three wooden steps to his porch and opened the screen door. It gave out a shrill shriek, indicating it was in desperate need of some oil. He unlocked the front door and entered his home. A rush of sticky warm air greeted him as he threw his keys down on the coffee table and headed to the kitchen.

Opening the fridge, he peered inside at the neat row of General Reserve beer. He grabbed one and wiped the frosty bottle across his forehead. The intense cold felt good against his damp brow. He began to uncap it when a thought popped into his head.

Do I really want this? he asked himself. He stared down at the beer and his eyes saw Samantha's face on the bottle; Samantha smiling at him at the diner and looking forward to their date. He put the beer back in the fridge and found a bottle of water trapped behind a box of baking soda. He removed it and took a long swallow of the cold water.

Not better than beer but it'll do, he thought.

He walked over to a thin cabinet and retrieved a bottle of aspirin, then removed two pills and swallowed them with another gulp of water. He was going to do his best to curb his drinking and pill intake. Looking up at the clock in his kitchen, he saw it was almost two thirty in the afternoon.

Time to wrap this up. Hopefully I can catch a nap before seeing Samantha, he thought as he walked to the living room and grabbed his keys.

John stepped out of his home and headed to his covered carport. Underneath sat his 1984 Bronco. The silver paint was starting to crack in some areas, but he loved his ride regardless. On top were three police lights and inside it, the Bronco was equipped with a radio transmitter. He opened the door and the sound of rusty springs and metal issued him a hello.

He climbed inside and made sure his mirrors were all right. His black New Orleans Saints hat was seated next to him and he placed it on his head.

The Bronco whined at first when he tried to start it and then fell silent. He tried it again and this time jammed his foot on the gas pedal, the Bronco roaring to life. He backed out of his shell driveway quickly as the tires sprayed the small white shells into the air.

He made his way to the main highway and took a right. The Reynolds lived on the side of Cypress Pass that backed up against the swamp.

John lit a cigarette and took a few drags before throwing it out the half-opened window. He'd known the Reynolds since he was a young boy, and William Reynolds had taken him fishing and alligator hunting numerous times.

John knew he liked his beer and he had made a deal with William that he wouldn't be arrested as long as he pulled over and slept off whatever was flowing through his system. John had received many calls about a man sleeping in his car on the side of the highway over the years.

He chuckled to himself lightly as he lit up another cigarette at the thought of William sleeping a few miles from his house, though he didn't pass him on the drive over.

The Reynolds' house was easy to spot as John pulled into the driveway. Unlike its neighbors, it was a large, shotgun-style home that had been built over two hundred years ago.

The dull green paint covering the house had faded badly in the sun. The red shutters however stood out like two red eyes and John could tell they'd been painted recently.

He noticed a familiar green sedan and a khaki van were parked next to one another and he breathed a sigh of relief.

Looks like the old bastard made it home after all, he thought. He exited the Bronco and stepped onto the wooden front porch. The old, dry wood creaked with each step as he walked to the front door.

A broken porch swing slowly rocked from side to side in the light breeze.

Weeds shot up from the cracks in the wood like small trees.

John removed his hat and wiped his forehead on his shirt sleeve.

Damn humidity, he thought as he pulled open the screen door and pounded on the light blue door behind it.

There was no answer. He listened for the sound of footsteps and muffled talking but he heard none. After a minute passed, he knocked again, and this time his knuckles hit the door with more authority.

"Mrs. Reynolds?" he called.

There was no answer. He walked over to the large square window and peered inside. A white curtain impeded his vision to the interior of the house.

"Mrs. Reynolds?" he called again. He tried first names next; shouting them. "Margerie! William?" He pounded on the door one last time.

There was still no answer.

They've got to be in the back, he thought and immediately felt foolish for thinking the worse.

He leapt off the porch and rounded the corner to the sprawling backyard. The home was backed up against a small plot of grass and the grass sloped down and gave way to the swamp. Mosquito-repelling torches lined the land where the grass met the swamp and a row of white sheets hung on a clothesline.

As the sheets gently flowed in the light wind, a flash of red caught John's eye. Suspicious as to what it was, he walked toward the source of his concern.

19

One of the white sheets was splattered with a red liquid. He touched a spot of the sticky fluid and brought his finger to his nose. The coppery smell filled his nostrils. He looked at the way the red dots made a pattern across the white sheet, almost like a spray.

A small puddle of blood was resting underneath the sheet and John removed his pistol from his holster with lightening quickness. He quickly glanced around the yard, confirming he was alone. He looked at the back of the house and noticed the back door was wide open.

Shitty job; that's how you get killed, he scolded himself for his rookie mistake of not checking his surroundings. He debated about running to his vehicle and calling for backup, but the adrenaline was coursing through his body and his mind was racing with possibilities as to how blood had been introduced to the white sheet. He walked toward the back door, doing his best to step silently in the dry grass.

As he walked up the steps, he saw a splotch of red on the wooden handrail. It was in the shape of a handprint.

He stepped carefully through the door and entered the laundry room. A lonely washing machine stood next to a sink and an ironing board that had been folded up and stacked against the wall. The smell of laundry detergent tickled his nose and John thought he might sneeze. Luckily, he was able to get the sensation under control. The laundry room gave way to a narrow hallway that was lit from the sun seeping in through the open back door.

His body blocked most of it and dim light offered just enough visibility. He could see off-colored patterns on the floor and walls. The hallway had three doors lining it; two on the left and one on the right. He approached each door with caution, passing two bedrooms and one bathroom, all unoccupied and all with doors open.

Various framed pictures hung on the hallway wall and John noticed several had been knocked off and now lay strewn on the floor. He carefully stepped over them as the hallway ended and led to a living room.

The red streaks continued to lead the way and they appeared to make a peculiar dripping pattern around the plaid couch and dark brown coffee table. He saw they were leading to the kitchen. He debated calling for William and Margerie again, but decided against it. If there was someone in the house who shouldn't be, he wanted to take them by surprise.

A slight grunting sound caused him to freeze. He readied his weapon and walked silently around the couch, coming into view of the kitchen. What he saw made him want to scream.

20

Blood and bits of flesh were strewn across the kitchen floor. John's eyes were fixed on the center of the kitchen where a gruesome sight was on display. Margerie Reynolds laid motionless on the green tile floor while a man was bent over her. John could hear the rip and tear of flesh as the man made snorting and chewing sounds. Margerie's head bobbed up and down with each bite from the man and her eyes stared blankly at the ceiling. Her mouth was frozen in a scream.

The man was wearing a brown plaid shirt and navy work pants. His brown boots were caked with mud and were slipping on the floor as he went in for each bite.

"Holy fucking shit…" John whispered.

The hunched-over man whipped around and his eyes locked onto John's. When he saw them, John saw they were a clouded white, like milk added to water. Blood was pouring from the man's mouth, and a ragged piece of flesh fell from his chomping teeth and onto the tile floor with a splat. Gore was smeared across the man's face and hair, and John thought he looked like one of those lions on the nature programs who would dive head first into a fat zebra meal. Although the man was covered in blood and tissue, John recognized him immediately.

"William?" John stammered in disbelief. "What the hell?"

William let out a loud moan, like an animal in pain, and stumbled toward John. The old man moved surprisingly fast and came at him with the speed of a jogger trying to run on two badly sprained ankles. William made a desperate lunge at John, but he was able to side step him, causing William to crash onto the hardwood floor.

"Stop, William! Stay down!" John ordered as he raised his pistol and aimed it.

William stumbled back to his feet and lumbered toward John again, his jaws snapping at the air around him.

"Freeze!" John yelled. "Don't make me do this!"

William didn't listen to the warning and made another lunge. John squeezed the trigger; the bullet ripping through William's chest. Instead of putting the old man down, he fell forward and onto John, knocking the sheriff to the floor. John's hand hit the floor, the gun falling to his side, his head almost landing on Margerie's lifeless body. He reached up and placed his hand on William's forehead, pushing the old man's face up and keeping the snapping jaws at bay.

The slick blood on the floor made it difficult for John to get leverage on William and his hand was slipping off the old man's forehead, so he quickly placed his forearm under William's chin and made a final attempt to roll the man over. He was finally able to get on top and he pushed off William with all his strength, rolling and coming up standing. William was trying to get up, but kept slipping in the blood pooled on the floor. John debated on making a try for his gun, but stopped when he saw what he knew was a very dead Margerie attempting to stand up.

"Holy shit," he gasped as the old woman pulled herself to a sitting position, then her knees. As she stood up, her liver and a row of intestines splattered the floor between her feet. She gave out a howl and began to move toward John; William was almost to his feet again as well.

Knowing that whatever was happening here, he was in way over his head, John turned and ran as fast as he could. He leapt over the couch and turned quickly into the hallway, running to the open back door.

Erupting from the house like a man shot from a cannon, he slipped on a slick patch of grass. Looking up, he could see the outlined forms of William and Margerie emerging from the hallway and into the laundry room. He got to his feet and ran to his Bronco, his hands frantically searching for his keys.

The howls of the Reynolds behind him were causing him to panic. He found his keys and the ignition key with no problem; it was the largest one on the ring. He opened the door and jumped inside, slamming the door behind him. He put the key into the ignition and turned it, and the Bronco's engine gave a whine, a faint stir, and then went silent.

He tried again but the result was the same. When he looked up and saw William and Margerie staggering quickly toward him, he tried again, praying whatever God oversaw old car engines would hear his prayer.

After a few shuffled paces, the old couple reached the Bronco. John couldn't help but think how glad he was that despite their marital problems of the past, William and Margerie had worked out their differences. Despite William eating her, they were a couple again.

William stumbled to the driver's side window and pressed his face against the glass; crimson blood oozed down the window. Margerie threw herself on top of the Bronco's hood and began smashing her face into the glass. John could see her teeth break off with each violent head bunt. He tried to start the Bronco again; it rumbled slightly and once again fell silent.

"Come on, baby, work for me," John pleaded as William's fists rained down on the window.

He pumped the gas and turned the ignition, yet again. The engine growled silently and then miraculously roared to life with a belch of smoke from the exhaust.

"Thank God!" he yelled, shifting the truck into reverse and backing out of the driveway with screeching tires.

Margerie flew off the hood and hit the ground with a sick thud. The Bronco's side mirror clipped William as the vehicle turned, causing the old man to fall to the ground. John slammed the truck into drive and pressed the gas pedal to the floor as hard as he could. As he checked his rearview mirror, he was relieved to see William and Margerie becoming quickly fading silhouettes in the background.

21

John reached his trembling hand forward and gripped his radio. He held it to his mouth and tried to speak but found the words stuck in his throat. His head was throbbing and his left arm was in pain from the tumble he'd taken on the kitchen floor.

He glanced down at the speedometer and noticed he was going a little over eighty miles an hour, so he lifted his foot off the accelerator and placed it gently onto the brake.

He brought the Bronco to a smooth stop on the shoulder of the highway facing the bayou. As he sat there, the engine idled softly. He hadn't driven very far, maybe half a mile, but he felt he was a good enough distance away from the Reynolds' home, so he pulled over and parked.

They were dead, he thought, but quickly pushed the foolish idea from his head. The only time he'd seen someone act like the Reynolds had was when he saw a police training video of someone with rabies. He took a quick look in his side mirror to make sure nothing was coming up behind him and brought the radio to his mouth one more time.

"Diane, this is John. I need backup to 3574 Highway 31, over!"

Several seconds passed and there was no reply. He let a few more seconds tick by, but there was still no response.

"Diane, this is John. Respond, over!"

No answer. The only sound he heard was his own heavy breathing. He reached into his pocket, grabbed his cigarettes, took one out, and placed it in his mouth. His hand was shaking so badly he needed to use his other hand to hold it still to light the cigarette. After a long drag, he began to settle down. He reached to his side and felt for his gun and felt nothing but his leg. He remembered he'd lost it in the kitchen during the scuffle.

"Fuck," he whispered.

He took another long drag of his cigarette, the nicotine starting to ease his nerves. He tried the radio again.

"Diane, come in. This is an emergency!"

Still no answer. Growing more annoyed with each passing second, he pulled his cell phone out of the center console and dialed the number for the police station. He'd just moved his finger over the **SEND** button when he heard the crack of a rifle.

22

John whipped his head to the side and tried to locate the source of the shot. He didn't have to search for very long when he saw a man emerge from behind a house not far up the road from where he was parked. The man was carrying a hunting rifle and appeared to be running as fast as he could. John saw he was short with a stocky build, and his little legs appeared to be having difficulty in moving his large frame. Suddenly, he stopped and faced the direction from where he had come.

John then saw what the man was running from. Another man dashed around the house and headed for where the stocky man was standing his ground. The other man shambled in the same way William and Margerie had been doing only minutes ago. The short man raised his rifle, took aim, and a second later a bullet tore a hole into the stumbling man's chest, dropping him to the ground.

"Holy shit!" John yelled as he drove in the direction of the altercation. In seconds he was parked on the green grass of the man's lawn and was running at the short man.

"Stop! Police!" John yelled, but the man paid him no attention.

The freshly shot man was flopping on the ground, trying his best to get up. John thought a gunshot wound like that might have severed his spine. The short man took aim one more time and sent a bullet through the wounded man's head. This time he stopped moving and laid on the ground as red blood flowed from his head like a river.

Then the man spun around and focused the 243 Winchester on John.

"Wait! Don't shoot!" John yelled as he reached his hands out to show the man he was harmless.

"Are you normal or are you one of them?"

"One of who? I'm the sheriff, damn it, just put the gun down!"

"I don't care if you're the fucking president. You better be normal!"

John looked down at himself and realized he was covered with the blood of William and Margerie.

"Just trust me, all right? I'm fine," John said softly, doing his best to calm the panic-stricken man.

The man started crying and lowered his gun.

"They killed my family. Six of those things, they came out of nowhere and killed them," the man sobbed harder as he finished the sentence.

"It's okay," John said sympathetically as he slowly walked toward him.

The man continued to cry and didn't notice that John was inching closer. When John was close enough, he kicked the gun out of the man's hand; the grip was loose and the gun fell to the ground. John pounced and placed the man in a headlock and wrestled him down with almost no resistance. Pinning him on his stomach, he brought the man's arms behind his back and handcuffed him.

"Wha-what're you doing?" the man stammered.

"It's for your protection. And mine."

John stood up and brushed off the grass that had stuck to the blood on his uniform.

"You do realize you just murdered a man?" John asked as he bent down and picked up the rifle.

"It's not a man! He was dead!" the man screamed, and a chill ran down John's spine.

The man was dead, just like William and Margerie, the voice inside his head whispered. John chose to ignore it.

"So you're telling me a dead man attacked you? Buddy, I've dealt with too much shit in the past few minutes to listen to this crap."

"It's true!" the man yelled back. "They're dead!"

John ignored him and walked back to his Bronco. He reached in, grabbed the radio, and tried the station one more time.

"Diane, this is John! Answer me, goddamn it!"

Still nothing. He threw the radio at the driver's seat in frustration, then turned and looked at the bayou, letting out a large breath. His head was starting to swim again with the thought of what the man had said.

They are dead, he repeated to himself. *No way, it's impossible.*

When he heard the man scream, John turned around and his doubts were immediately challenged.

23

William and Margerie Reynolds were quickly staggering their way across the lawn to the cuffed man lying helplessly on the ground. William was in front of his wife by several feet, and to John's horror, he could see Margerie's right foot bent completely to the side, a small white bone protruding from her leg. She appeared to be walking on it like a cane.

"Fucking shoot them!" the man screamed at John.

John ran closer to the shambling couple and raised the rifle. Neither seemed to notice him, their eyes fixed on the easy meal in front of them.

"William! Margerie! Freeze!"

The warning was ignored. William was closest to the handcuffed man and he fell on him and sank his teeth into the man's plump shoulder. The man screamed as William removed a fat chunk of meat.

"Goddamn it, shoot them, you idiot!" the man screamed again as he tried to flail away from William.

John took aim, fired, and sent a bullet into William's side. The impact knocked William's thin body off the man and onto the ground. John then turned his sights onto Margerie and aimed for her left knee. He fired and the force of the round blew her knee out and she crumpled to the ground, making no attempt to cradle her fall. After a few seconds, she lifted her head. Her eyes were still locked on the man as she used both hands to crawl toward him, her mouth open and drool foaming out of the corners.

"You've got to be shitting me," John whispered in disbelief.

"You have to shoot them in the head!" the man screamed. "Hurry! Do it!"

William raised himself off the ground and turned his attention to John. He curled his lips in a snarl at the person who had interrupted his meal. His white eyes were locked onto John and he staggered forward, both his arms outstretched. Letting out a loud groan, he lunged forward.

With a shot worthy of the Army Rangers, John sent a bullet right between William's eyes. A mist of red exploded out the back of his skull and John could have sworn he saw Scarface, then the vision dissipated. William stood for a second before crumpling to the ground, this time not moving. John walked over to Margerie who was still making her best effort to get to the cuffed man and put a bullet in the back of her head. She slumped over, still.

"I told you," the man said angrily. "It's the head that does it."

"Shut up," was all John could think to say. He turned and ran back to the Bronco and tried the radio again. "Diane answer me!" he pleaded.

Silence. He threw the radio against the seat again, this time a little harder, then walked back to the man.

"Are you okay to walk?"

"What the fuck do you think? Just help me up!" the man snapped.

John grabbed him by the arm and lifted him to his feet. He cried out in pain and John realized he'd grabbed the arm with the bite on his shoulder. John took a second to look at the wound. A patch of the man's camouflage shirt was missing where William had locked his teeth. A piece of shoulder, about as big as a fist, was also missing. Bright red blood was flowing from the gap. John removed the handcuffs and attached them to his belt loop. The man rubbed his wrists and then started to bring a hand to touch his shoulder before John stopped him.

"Don't touch it," he said and the man drew his hand back. "You gotta name?"

"Charlie, Charlie Simmons."

"Do you have any more ammo, Charlie?"

"Yeah, in the house."

"Show me," John said, and Charlie led the way.

24

They entered the small house and John looked at Charlie.

"Where?" he asked.

"In the bedroom, last room on the left."

John walked down the hallway and Charlie followed closely behind him. As they passed a room on the right, John came to a stop. Three bodies were strewn about the room, surrounded by a sea of carnage. For a moment, John saw the dead soldiers lying behind the pallet of sand bags. He quickly snapped back to reality and focused on one woman and two young children. He turned back to Charlie who was covering his face. John could see the tears streaming down his cheeks. He entered the room and Charlie moved past him. He went to where the woman laid on the bed and cradled her head in his arms.

"Belinda, I'm so sorry," he sobbed.

John looked at the three corpses and noticed bite marks on their limbs and throats. He also noticed a clean bullet hole in each one's head.

"They came back," Charlie choked as he lightly stroked his dead wife's hair. "Those things killed them and they came back. My wife, my son, and my beautiful little girl. All came back! And then they tried to kill me! They didn't even recognize me anymore. And I pleaded with them to remember me. God knows how hard I pleaded with them. But it wasn't them anymore. I had to shoot them. I couldn't let them be like that."

"I'm going to the bedroom to get the ammo," John said softly. Charlie nodded his head in acknowledgment, never taking his eyes away from his wife.

John entered the bedroom and immediately walked over to an old wooden dresser. He opened the drawers and dumped the contents onto the bed. He didn't find what he was looking for. He tried his hardest not to look at the picture perched on top of the dresser; a picture of two children fishing and their dad looking on in fatherly satisfaction. John saw a nightstand and opened the drawer. He found some hand cream and a box of tissues. He went to the night stand on the other side of the bed and found a pair of glasses and a bible.

"Damn it!" he yelled as he let his frustration get the better of him.

He walked over to a small closet and opened it. On the top shelf was an empty gun case.

"Jackpot," he muttered and pulled the box down.

A 9mm Glock was sitting atop the foam padding. He popped the clip out and saw it was full. He also saw another clip fully loaded and a box of about fifty bullets. He noticed they were hollow points. A box of twenty rifle rounds also sat in the case and he snatched them up. He closed the case and sat back down on the bed.

Looking down at the faded wooden floor, he took several deep breaths and tried to comprehend what was happening. He reached into his pocket and removed his cell phone. He was going to dial the police station but noticed the NO SIGNAL displayed in the top left corner. He shook his head and stood up.

Gotta love technology, he thought as he placed the phone and ammo into his pockets and left the bedroom.

John walked back into the room where Charlie's family lay and saw he was now holding his young son. John removed a cigarette. Compared to Charlie, John was a model of composure, but his hand still shook slightly as he lit his cigarette. He could hear Charlie whispering to himself. Tears were still running down his face.

"Just shoot 'em in the head," Charlie whispered, repeating the phrase over and over.

As John watched, Charlie was starting to make him nervous. "Come on. We have to get going," he said, wishing he didn't have to be so heartless.

"But my family, I can't leave them here," Charlie choked, doing his best to hold back any new tears.

"Charlie, I'm so sorry for your loss. But I don't know what the hell is going on. A moment ago you told me the dead were attacking you and I thought you were crazy. Now I don't know what to think. The only thing I do know is that there's something not right and these people attacking us may be sick, and you were bit by one of them! We need to get you to the clinic now and have Doc Adams look at you, and I need to get to the police station and find out why my calls aren't being answered. So please, let's just get out of here."

Charlie hesitated for a moment and then kissed the top of his boy's head, then he crawled over to the little girl and lightly kissed her cheek. Finally, he walked over to his wife and kissed her lips softly. He began to cry softly again as John put a hand on his back and helped guide him out the room and out of the house.

25

John exited the house quietly and looked around. Seeing the coast was clear, he motioned for Charlie to follow him. He handed Charlie back his rifle and he held onto the 9mm. He was more capable with a handgun anyway.

The two men quickly walked toward the Bronco and John opened the passenger side door for Charlie, who winced in pain as he tried to pull himself up with his injured shoulder.

"Hold on, I'll help," John said as he helped lift him into the seat.

John ran around and hopped into the Bronco. He started the engine and began to make his way toward Downtown Cypress Pass.

"Where are we going?" Charlie asked.

"We're going to the police station first to try and figure this all out. I'll call the clinic when we get there and have Doc Adams come to us."

John noticed Charlie had short black hair which was starting to bald in the front. He also had a pudgy face that resembled a bulldog with fat cheeks and a slight under-bite. John looked at his cell phone again; there was still no signal. He reached down for his pack of cigarettes and found it empty.

"Just great," he grumbled and tossed the empty pack out the window. He tried the radio again but still got no response. Charlie had stopped crying and was sitting back and looking at the bayou in silence. John turned on the Bronco's radio and found nothing but static.

"How're you feeling?" John asked Charlie, who didn't respond. His chest was slowly rising up and down and John figured he must have fallen asleep or gone into shock.

Doc Adams can worry about this in a few minutes, John thought as he sped down the highway.

As downtown approached, John gazed out of his window and looked over the houses he was passing by. The first few he came across yielded nothing of interest. A few miles later, that changed. As he passed a white, shotgun-style home with a red door, he noticed a woman running across the lawn. Behind her, two men in blood-stained overalls were giving chase. The scene reminded him of wolves after a rabbit. He debated stopping and even removed his foot off the gas and started to press the brake when he talked himself out of it.

These people are crazy, he thought, though he hated himself a little more for not stopping.

The sun was already starting to melt into the bayou and dusk was approaching. He looked at the clock on the dashboard and saw it was a little after six. Charlie made a gurgled, choking sound from beside him.

"Charlie, you all right?" John asked as he noticed the bite on the man's shoulder.

The ragged hole was now a festering wound. Red tinted foam spilled from the opening, and around it the skin, was turning an off-green.

"Jesus Christ, Doc Adams is going to have a time with you."

Suddenly, Charlie sat straight up. His eyes were fixed forward and John could see a string of saliva slowly pouring from the corner of his mouth. Then Charlie's head turned toward John.

"Just sit back. We will be at the station soon..." was all he could say before Charlie let out a chilling howl and lunged at John.

26

John could feel the hot breath of Charlie's snapping mouth near his face as he struggled to hold the man off. Charlie let out a horrible cry that sounded like the death rattle of a slaughterhouse cow and continued trying to maul John's face. John managed to get his right hand under Charlie's throat and held him at bay as he struggled to steer the Bronco with his left. Then he felt Charlie grab his shirt sleeve and pull him closer to his greedy mouth.

In a desperate motion, John shot his right hand forward with all his might. He could feel Charlie's jugular give way and feel the bend of cartilage and snap of tendons. Under normal circumstances, Charlie should now be choking to death while his lungs filled with blood, but instead, he pressed the attack. A feeling washed over John. A feeling he hadn't experienced since he was a soldier trapped inside a terrorist bunker: fear.

The fear didn't linger long, and John knew his time was about to run out unless he did something to stop Charlie.

Swerving the Bronco to the left, he then swung hard to the right. The sudden shift in momentum sent Charlie crashing against the passenger door, giving John the break he needed. Grabbing the 9mm, he lined up Charlie's head from no more than a foot away and sent a hollow point streaking toward the man's skull. The bullet made contact and the result was a shower of blood and brain matter splattering the dashboard. The passenger window shattered as well.

John turned his attention back to the road just in time to see a car barreling toward him. He cut the wheel quickly, narrowly missing the car, but hitting the ditch that ran parallel to the highway. He could feel the Bronco go airborne and he wrapped his arms around the steering wheel to try to prevent himself from being thrown while still clutching his gun. Charlie's lifeless corpse was flung through the open window, as the Bronco hit the ground hard and began to roll. After making three full turns it came to a smoking stop, resting on its side in a cloud of dust.

27

Samantha and Simone held on to each other as they sat on the floor of a broken refrigeration unit. The unit had broken years ago, and instead of getting it fixed, Simone had ordered a new walk-in cooler and turned the broken one into dry storage. Little did she know that one day the broken unit would keep her alive.

They had witnessed the outbreak from behind the diner counter. As the madness spilled in, Samantha had grabbed Simone and the two fled into the unit. The unit had a unique safety feature in that there was no lock on the outside, the manufacture's way of making sure no one could be locked in, but it wasn't hard to jury-rig a lock for inside.

They held each other as Simone lightly sobbed into her apron. They tried to remain silent, but the occasional scream followed by the crash of dishes and silverware made them jump. A few times, Samantha had to clamp her hand over Simone's mouth to stifle a panicked scream. Darkness and the stale smell of cardboard surrounded them as their only source of light came from the Zippo lighter that was shaking in Simone's hand. With every sound echoing from outside the unit, her hand would jump, causing the light to flicker, which cast eerie shadows across the wall.

"Turn it off," Samantha whispered to Simone.

Simone shook her head as the tears streamed down her wrinkled cheeks.

"Simone, please."

But Simone didn't hear her. She closed her eyes and began quietly reciting the Lord's Prayer. Just as she was asking the Big Guy to lead her not into temptation, a loud thud was heard as something came into contact with the door. Both women stared at the door and then each other as they slowly backed away deeper inside the unit.

Samantha leaned her face forward and blew out the lighter. As soon as she did this, she brought her hand over Simone's mouth and muffled the scream before it could happen. Darkness swallowed them both.

The thumping on the door continued, but to Samantha's relief it didn't sound like someone was trying to get in. It was more like someone, or something, was bumping into the door over and over again. Samantha gazed at the bottom of the door, where a small crack was present between the door and the floor where the rubber gasket had peeled off from age.

Multiple shadows appeared, pacing back and forth.

28

Mike had called Kelly's cell phone seven times before finally giving up. He was so excited by the cash John gave him that he couldn't contain himself. When she didn't answer the first three times, he figured she was probably in the shower. When she didn't call him back, he figured she was drying her hair, and when he called her four more times, he concluded that she had her phone on silent and couldn't hear it. He tried their home phone a few times but there was no answer there either.

She's probably taking a nap, he thought, knowing she was prone to afternoon naps. She was always dead to the world when she took them, too. He was excited that he would get to show her the money and see her reaction in person, but his excitement left him as he turned into his driveway and spotted his front door open.

Worry began to set in as he jumped out of his car and ran up the three steps that led to his porch. He almost barged in when he remembered his police training. He removed his pistol, flipped the safety off, and entered his home. He walked into the living room and looked around cautiously. Everything seemed to be normal.

"Kelly?" he called out.

A muffled scream from the second floor answered him. Gripping the gun tighter, he ran up the stairs and came to a stop when he reached the final step.

In the hallway was a man. His left hand was slapping at the door to the hall bathroom. Every time his hand made contact, Kelly would let out a scream that was muffled by the door. The man was shirtless and barefoot, the only article of clothing on him a pair of loose-fitting jeans.

"Freeze asshole!" Mike screamed as rage and adrenalin flooded his bloodstream.

He raised the gun and aimed it. The man had stopped pounding on the door and was now turning to face him. Mike almost dropped his gun when he saw the rest of the guy's body. A ragged stump with a jagged piece of white bone, protruding like a spike, was all that remained of the man's left arm. The intruder issued a chilling cry as he lurched quickly toward Mike, who responded by sending a bullet right through the man's head, dropping him instantly. The body fell limp to the floor and Mike was at the bathroom door before the corpse had settled. He tried the handle but it was locked, so he put his face against the door and talked as calmly as he could, even though his heart was racing.

"Kelly, baby, it's me. Open the door, you're safe now," he said softly.

He could hear her lightly crying.

"Baby, it's okay. I took care of the guy who broke in. He can't hurt you now, I promise."

He heard the door unlock and slowly creak open, showing him his wife. Her white tank top was speckled with drops of red blood and her jean shorts appeared to have been ripped at the pocket on the right side. Her tan skin was glistening with sweat and her brown eyes were a blotchy red. Her brown hair was a mess around her pretty, full face and the premature graying speckled her twenty-eight year old head.

Kelly leapt into Mike's arm and hugged him hard. She caught sight of the body on the floor and immediately jumped back.

"It's okay, he's dead," Mike assured her and led her to their bedroom across the hall.

They sat on the bed for a moment in silence as Kelly continued to hug him. He could feel her breathing start to slow and her heartbeat begin to return to its normal rhythm.

"What happened?" he asked.

"I heard someone at the door and I thought it was you," she said, and paused for a moment. Before Mike could ask her to continue, she said, "I opened the door and he was just standing on our porch. I saw his arm and thought there must have been some accident. I didn't know what to say because he just stood there with no expression. He didn't even seem to be in any pain. He just stared at me for a second and then jumped on me. I was able to push him off and I ran up the stairs. I ran into the bathroom and locked the door. I don't know how long I was in there, but he didn't go away. He just kept beating on the door. Then you came…" she trailed off, not needing to finish the story.

"I didn't want to shoot him," Mike said. "But he was trying to hurt you and he was in our house. I wasn't taking any chances. But the way he acted is what's really bothering me. I told him to freeze and instead he came at me. It was like he didn't care that I had a gun drawn on him. Like he didn't even see it. All he saw was me."

The two sat on the bed and tried to take it all in. After a few minutes passed, Mike finally broke the silence. "We should probably get to the station. I'll give John a ring on the way over. I'm sure I'll have a ton of paperwork to fill out. I never shot any one before. I don't know what to do next."

They got up from the bed and made their way downstairs. The first thing Mike saw was that the door to the house was still open. The second thing he noticed was a group of four people slowly walking across his lawn. He went to the doorway and watched them. It looked like a group of kids, no more than twelve-years-old, and a fat woman that could have been one of their mothers. As Mike's large frame filled the doorway, the four kids began to awkwardly jog at him. It looked as if they were just learning how their legs worked; the fat woman resembling a sheepherder leading the kids his way. One of the runners let out a howl and a chill ran down Mike's spine. It sounded like the man who he'd just killed.

"Kelly, get up stairs, now!" he shouted and looked away from the oncoming people to warn her. It was a mistake.

When he turned around and went to close the door, the body of the obese woman was suddenly there, blocking his way. With her arms outstretched, she crashed down on Mike and he felt his breath leave him. He could hear Kelly scream as the large woman groaned and snapped her jaws at his exposed neck. Mike grabbed the collar of her flower print blouse and was able to keep her face away from him. Spittle and blood began to pour from her mouth, to pool onto his navy-blue deputy shirt. He could feel his grip on her slipping.

Suddenly, Kelly brought the end of an iron fire poker on top of the woman's skull and he heard a sick crack as the woman went limp. He rolled her off him and jumped to his feet.

When he looked at the doorway, he saw that the four kids were now only a few yards away from the steps leading to his front door. Behind them, he made out the shape of more people heading in his direction.

Kelly was behind him, staring at the woman on the floor, the poker hanging loosely in her hand.

"Kelly! Run!" he ordered and pushed her toward the stairs.

She was halfway up them as Mike began his ascent. Luckily for him, the fat woman had fallen right at the doorway and served as a speed bump for the four kids, all of them tumbling to the floor, the action resembling a TV sitcom.

"Get to the bedroom!" Mike yelled as he made it up the stairs.

Kelly turned sharply into their bedroom and Mike was right behind her. He slammed the door closed and locked it. He could hear the crash of glass and the sounds of footsteps stomping in the living room. Then the footsteps were heard echoing in the stairwell.

"Fuck-fuck-fuck, think-think-think," he whispered to himself while pacing the room. Adrenalin was suffusing his system and he was so wired he wanted to scream. Fight or flight was never so much in effect. His thoughts were interrupted as the first intruder slammed into the thin bedroom door. He could hear the frame crack.

"The roof!" he screamed. "We need to get on the roof!"

Mike took a deep breath and slid their heavy oak dresser in front of the door. He hoped it would buy them the time they needed; just a few precious, lifesaving seconds.

Kelly ran to the window and opened it. Outside was a small balcony that she had placed a few potted plants on. She climbed through the opening and stood on top of the iron guardrails that surrounded it. Using all her strength, she hoisted herself onto the roof and gazed out at the land surrounding their home. Her head was spinning as she counted the people making their way toward her, as if a party had been announced and she was hosting it. She stopped when she was certain the number exceeded a hundred.

Once Kelly was out the window, Mike raced over to the bed. He lifted up the mattress and grabbed the revolver stashed there for emergencies. Kelly had wanted him to get a lock-box for it but with no kids in the house, he didn't think it was a necessity.

The pounding on the door was getting louder and with each bang came the sound of cracking wood. As the first hand smashed through the door, Mike made his way out the window and onto the roof.

He sat next to Kelly and the two stared at the people lumbering across their lawn. Tears were running down her face and Mike placed an arm around her. He shoved the revolver in her open hand.

"Just point and pull the trigger. You got six shots, baby, so make them count."

He gestured with his head, indicating to Kelly where she should direct her aim.

"If someone comes at you, don't screw around, there's too many of them. Just aim for the head, baby. One shot and it's a guarantee they'll go down for good. We can't afford to just wound them. But if you can't hit that small a target, go for the chest, but we've spent time at the range together, I know you can do it."

She nodded, understanding. "What's wrong with everyone? Why are they doing this?"

Mike shrugged, sweat running down his forehead. "I don't know. Maybe some terrorist put a virus in the drinking water or it's some kind of mass hysteria…drugs maybe. It doesn't matter, all that does is that you stay safe." He held her hand, squeezing it gently. "Stay here and watch that balcony. If one of them tries to get on it, shoot them. I'm gonna check the other side of the house."

"What about the ones in our house now?"

He shook his head. "That dresser is pretty heavy; it should keep them from getting into our bedroom. You'll hear it if they knock it over. And if they do get past it, they might try to climb up here like we did. I'll be right back, I want to check on something." He kissed her, stood up, and walked to the side of the house overlooking the porch. When he looked down, his heart sank. Staring back at him was about thirty people. When they saw him, they began to wail and moan as they stretched their arms toward him. Their hoarse voices made him shudder, but worse was the intense look of their cloudy eyes; there gazes were so dead, yet so primal. It filled him with dread.

Walking back to Kelly, he sat down beside her, and placed an arm around her to try and comfort her; she was lightly shaking. He looked out at the massive crowd that was forming.

There's so many of them, he thought. He didn't know how this was possible, but he knew it wasn't going to end well. How could it? Cypress Pass was just a small town, but there seemed to be hundreds of messed-up people surrounding his home with more coming from various directions. The ones nearest the house were moaning and wailing, and it reminded Mike of a decomposing mosh pit. And the smell, like meat left in the sun for too long, along with the odor of spilled blood.

He rested his pistol on his lap and pulled Kelly closer to him.

"What's happening? This can't be real," she whispered.

"I don't know, babe. I just don't know," he replied and stared at the blood-covered crowd, some with what sure appeared to be mortal wounds suffered from what looked like savage animal attacks.

Suddenly a thought crossed his mind. It was so absurd, so unbelievable, but at the moment it made perfect sense. So much sense that he almost let out a laugh at the absurdity of it.

"They look like they're dead," he stated.

"Dead? Really? That's impossible, this isn't a horror movie, Mike, this is real life." She gave him a look like he'd just gone crazy.

"Well, it may sound crazy but that's my guess," he replied and pointed to an old man with half his throat torn out. "Look at that guy on the right. There's no way he could live with half his throat missing." He pointed to a housewife with curlers in her hair. The pale woman was missing an arm, tendrils of muscle and sinew hanging lazily. "And her, she should have bled out a long time ago."

Kelly paused for a moment, considering Mike's suggestion. Everything had happened so fast, she never had time to take it all in. "The apocalypse? The end of days? The Bible said that at the end the dead would walk," she said.

"I don't think the Bible meant they would walk and try to kill and eat people," he said and pointed to a spot where a zombie was carrying a severed leg, chewing on it with what appeared to be true gusto.

"I don't know what God's will is, Mike."

"Well if this is His will, He is a pretty fucked-up guy."

They both went silent then, each thinking on what had been said. Mike knew Kelly was very religious, much so more than he was. He knew he'd probably crossed a line, but he didn't really care. In his mind he wasn't so sure how he felt about the idea of

God at the moment. He thought of a saying, 'there are no atheists in a fox hole.'

"We still haven't had kids, and if this keeps going and no one comes to help us, maybe never…" she said, breaking down a little. So far she'd been strong but now that she had time to gather her thoughts, the true horror of the situation was sinking in.

Mike hugged her closer to him and lightly kissed the top of her head.

"Kelly, don't talk like that. It's not over yet," he said quietly, trying to reassure himself as well as her. "We still have plenty of time for kids. And one day, when we're all sitting around the dinner table, we can tell them about the time their mom and dad got stuck on the top of their house by a pack of crazy people."

Below, the crowd was climbing over one another, a few getting on the shoulders of smaller ones to try and reach the roof, but so far, none had even gotten close. There was a trellis to the side that could be used as ladder but none had noticed it or were too stupid to understand what it was.

"I love you, Mike," she said as the crash of the dresser blocking their bedroom door came to them as it was knocked aside.

"I love you, too," he said.

They both gripped their guns tightly and waited for the first zombie to reach the balcony.

29

The Bronco's rear, driver's side wheel was still slowly spinning in the air as the vehicle lay upside down. All of the windows had been smashed, shattered glass sprinkled around the truck like snow, the shards catching the sun. A thin wisp of black smoke rose slowly into the air.

John emerged from the wreckage slowly. He could feel his body protesting his movements, flashes of pain filling his head, as he crawled slowly through the broken glass. A large gash on his forehead produced a steady stream of blood, which poured into his eyes, causing them to burn and his vision to become a blurry red.

He stood up carefully, making sure no bones were broken. Bringing his arm up, he wiped the blood from his face. For a brief moment, he saw his military Humvee flipped over, and his two dead friends staring at him with lifeless eyes.

He blinked a few times and the ghostly image from the past went away. He walked back to the wrecked Bronco and peered inside. The rifle was still there. Finally some luck was on his side. He reached in and grabbed it, slung it over his shoulder, searched the vehicle one more time before leaving; everything appeared smashed and worthless.

Turning away from the ruined Bronco, he began his trek up the highway and soon saw a small wooden sign which displayed: *DOWNTOWN: 5 Miles*.

"Shit," he growled as he limped down the highway.

Since the houses of Cypress Pass were so spread apart, John didn't reach the first home until he'd limped a little over half a mile. He hoped for a car to be in the driveway but had no luck, so he moved on. He was also praying a car would come along and maybe he could hitch a ride to the station, but no one was on the highway today—not one. Which seemed odd when he thought about it, but he wasn't in the right frame of mind to consider it at the moment.

He was a little into his second mile when he came across a light lavender farm house. Sitting in the driveway was an old-looking Ford F-150 with rust on the sides and a tennis ball on the antenna. John walked up the driveway and approached the truck. His rifle was drawn and he was searching for the slightest movement or sound. A thin stream of blood trickled down his arm. The paint of the red truck had faded for the most part, and as he got closer, he saw more patches of rust eating away at the bed.

He grabbed the driver's side door handle but it was locked. He peered inside the dusty window but no keys were visible, as if it would be that easy. He debated smashing the window with the rifle and trying to hot wire the truck, but quickly shot the idea down. He didn't want to break a window in case he ran into anymore of the crazy people again. Well, that and he didn't know how to hotwire a vehicle.

Figuring the keys might be inside the house, he walked up the porch and tried the front door. It lightly creaked as it swung forward. John walked inside and did a quick scan of the interior.

"Hello, anyone home? I had an accident and could use some help," he called out loudly, so that anyone in the house would know he was there.

When there was no answer, he cautiously made his way to the kitchen, which was adjacent to the living room. Walking over to the sink, he scrubbed his face with cold water. The wound on his forehead burned as the water splashed on it. Picking up a roll of paper towels, he dried his face, then held a wad of towels to his forehead to stop the bleeding.

Limping to the refrigerator, he opened it and a slight smile crept across his face. Nestled behind a gallon of milk was a six pack of beer. He reached in and grabbed a bottle. Twisting off the cap, he emptied the entire beer in a few quick gulps. The sensation of the cold liquid and the carbonated bubbles were like heaven, so he reached in and grabbed another and greedily drank it down. His stomach gurgled as the cold alcohol settled and John realized he was hungry—starving actually.

On the shelf below the beer was what looked like pot roast, the meat firmly set in place by gelatinous gravy and fat. He grabbed it and began wolfing down the meat like it was his last meal. The meat was salty and pretty tender for being cold and he was even a little surprised when he finished off the entire thing.

Closing the fridge door, he leaned against the counter. He was just about to think of where to begin looking for the keys when he spotted them. In the corner of the kitchen, near a side entrance door, was a little shelf for mail. Under the shelf were two hooks: one had a dog leash and the other had a ring of keys. John grabbed the keys, and sure enough, there was one with the Ford symbol on it.

About damn time, he thought, happy with his run of good luck, until a light moan and the sound of something being dragged across the floor made his heart drop.

John grabbed his 9mm and slowly began walking toward the source of the noise. Upon exiting the kitchen, he saw a teenage boy dragging himself across the carpet. The zombie's legs appeared to be broken. One was turned sideways at the knee and the other had a jagged piece of shin bone protruding through an oozing hole of pus and blood. The boy reached one hand toward John as the other slowly dragged the mangled body across the floor.

To John's horror, he recognized the boy.

"Chris..." John muttered.

Chris Lowery was only thirteen-years-old. He'd cut John's grass a few times during the summer to earn some money for a dog. John had always thought he was a good kid. But the thing crawling toward him now sure wasn't Chris.

Suddenly, the piece of bone sticking out of Chris' leg became lodged in the carpet. The boy tried to move forward but found he couldn't. John saw what had happened and stared in disbelief.

He doesn't even know why he's stuck, he thought.

John took a deep breath and walked over to the couch. He grabbed a thick, brown pillow and walked behind Chris, who made a feeble attempt to grab him, but John was well out of reach. John placed his boot on the back of Chris' neck and forced his head to the floor. He placed the pillow firmly on the back of the boy's head and then jammed the gun down into it. He pulled the trigger, the pillow muffling the loud bang. Chris' arms shot to the side and he dropped to the floor, going still.

"Goddamn it," John said softly.

He debated exploring the rest of the house but doubted he would come across anything he really needed. He also didn't want to encounter any more people like Chris. He went back to the kitchen and grabbed a beer for the road.

Don't drink and drive, kids, he thought and let out a chuckle. He wondered if the chuckle was meant he was cracking up, but then he stopped himself and felt a little better. Sometimes you had to laugh or cry and he'd chosen the former. When he was about to leave, he saw the phone hanging on the wall. Wondering how he could have missed it, he picked up the receiver and placed it to his ear. There was a dial tone. He quickly punched in the number to the police station and the phone began to ring, and ring, and ring. After the seventh ring, he hung up. Taking a sip of beer, he walked out the kitchen and left the house.

He walked to the F-150 and placed the key in the door, the lock popping open. Climbing in, he closed the door behind him, making sure to lock it. The truck was relatively clean on the inside. A few fast food wrappers littered the floor and covered some empty beer cans. John placed the key in the ignition and the engine roared to life. He tried the radio but like before was greeted with only white noise and static.

"Why me?" he asked and placed his throbbing head on the wheel. At least his head wound had stopped bleeding.

He perked up suddenly, convinced he'd heard a noise. Looking around, he saw nothing. Preparing to back out of the driveway, he adjusted the rearview mirror, only to find the face of a zombie greeting him in the reflection. As his heart began to beat faster and he prepared for yet another fight, he realized he was looking at his own reflection.

"Jesus Christ…" he whispered and felt his face.

The cut on his forehead had formed a jagged line that disappeared into his hair line. There was a purple bruise around his left eye, and his lips were swollen. His right eye was deeply bloodshot.

"I look like one of them," he muttered.

He put the truck in reverse and slowly backed out of the gravel driveway. When he reached the highway, he made a left turn and headed toward downtown. Before he'd driven very far, he thought of Mike and realized he needed to get him, so he made a quick left at the next street and drove to collect his deputy.

30

Mike carefully peered over the roof and looked down at the small balcony. None of the walking dead who had entered the bedroom had made it out the window yet, but he knew it was only a matter of time.

As he stretched his head over, the sea of the undead saw him and it whipped them into a ravenous frenzy. Their cloudy eyes locked on him and their disfigured mouths snapped and drooled in anticipation. Mike backed away before they got too excited.

"Maybe we should try and make a run for it," Kelly said, taking Mike by surprise. "We could climb down the other side of the house where the ivy lattice is. You said there weren't that many on the other side, right?"

Mike looked at her and then looked back at the growing number of dead.

"I don't know, babe. It seems like suicide. I don't even think that lattice would support me."

"Then maybe I should go and get help for you."

"No way, that's a horrible idea. You just need to calm down. Help will be here soon. I'm sure of it."

The two sat silent for a moment. Mike could see fresh tears streaming down Kelly's tan cheeks.

"Where are they coming from?" she asked. "They don't even look like people from around here. Some are wearing business suits! I didn't think anyone outside of the mayor even owned a suit."

"Maybe they're coming from other towns," Mike suggested, guessing.

"Well, if they are from other towns, then we're seriously *screwed*." She hissed the last word, signifying how upset she truly was.

A loud crash caused both Mike and Kelly to jump. It was the glass on the window which led to the balcony. It had shattered as bodies attempted to get through the small opening.

"Kelly, get behind me!" Mike ordered as he drew his gun.

Mike's eyes were locked on to the balcony a few feet below him. The first zombie that dared poke its head out was getting it blown off. Further below him, on the ground, the mass of zombies shrieked and howled.

"Shut the fuck up!" he screamed, but this only caused them to moan louder.

Then an arm with no hand emerged from the window. The limb was thin and pale white and had been sliced to ribbons by the broken glass. As the zombie got its body halfway out the window, Mike saw it was a woman. He couldn't see her face, but by her hair and clothes she looked to be well into her seventies. He didn't hesitate, and squeezed the trigger on his gun. A half-second later, a bullet went straight through her head. She fell to the side, her body landing on the railing and becoming stuck. Her front half dangled limply in the air. Mike could see her body shift forward each time the dead behind her pushed as they tried to get onto the balcony.

Then, slicing through the loud moans, the sound of a car horn made him turn his attention away from the zombie log jam.

A faded red Ford F-150 came barreling down the street. As the truck got closer, Mike recognized the man sitting behind the wheel and a smile creased his lips, relief flooding his body. "Holy shit! John! John! Up here! We're up here!" Mike screamed and waved his arms like a lunatic.

Soon Kelly was joining him, the two yelling and waving to get John's attention. The dead didn't notice the truck yet, too preoccupied with the show atop the roof.

John sped toward the house and made a wide circle around it. He swerved to miss a few of the zombies, especially a rather large man who might have done more damage to the truck if he was hit. The back side of the house was virtually zombie free except for a group of six hugging the side of the home. He accelerated toward them, buckling his seat belt before he made impact.

"What the hell…"Mike said as John drove straight for the group.

John plowed into them and the impact of the truck sent two bodies flying away like ragdolls with shattered limbs. Three more were thrown into the air and another was flattened beneath the spinning wheels.

As the Ford lurched to a stop, John opened the driver's door and tried to jump out, but the seatbelt prevented him. He quickly unbuckled it. Pieces of arms, legs, and torso's peppered the front hood. A head had hit the windshield and burst like a rotten melon, leaving behind blood and gore. He'd brought the Ford to a stop so close to the house that the passenger side mirror had been torn off.

"Come on!" John yelled as he got out of the truck. "While it's still clear!"

"Kelly, let's go!" Mike yelled as the two made their way to the edge and began to slowly descend the lattice. "This is our only chance."

Mike tried not to think about his weight, or that every piece of the lattice he touched seemed to bend and crack. He also tried not to think about how much he'd bitched about having to put it up, all so Kelly could grow some damn ivy on the side of the house. He was glad he'd listened to her now.

"Come on! Hurry!" John yelled.

Two zombies lurched up to the Ford and awkwardly climbed into the rear bed. Both were so damaged, they literally fell apart as they moved. Their eyes were fixed on John like they were wild animals and he was the prey. He put a bullet in each one of their skulls and dragged them out of the bed.

Mike was the first to reach the Ford and he jumped from the lattice and into the rear bed, his boots landing with a loud thud. Kelly still had more than halfway to go.

"Jesus, Kelly speed it up!" John yelled, his eyes fixed on the mass of undead that were quickly approaching them.

"Just jump, Kelly! I got you!" Mike yelled.

He wasn't sure if she jumped or slipped, but a second later she came tumbling down. He caught her in his big arms, bending his knees to absorb her weight.

He quickly put her down and grabbed his gun from where he'd lodged it behind his back.

John was standing in the open driver's side door as he fired into the advancing dead, each shot dropping a zombie. Mike began firing wildly, many of his shots ending up in the torso of a zombie who didn't seem to notice.

"Guys sit down and hold on, it's time to go!" John yelled and closed the driver's door, put the transmission into reverse, and backed away from the house.

"Go! Go! Go!" Mike yelled as he and Kelly hit the bottom of the bed and held on to the sides, the Ford lurching and shaking.

When John was clear of the side of the house, he put the truck in drive, the Ford lurching forward to swing around the yard and back onto the road. He swerved the Ford hard to the left to avoid a large crowed of undead, and seconds later, the undead mob was left behind.

31

John was panicking. All the gore from the zombies he'd run down was now splattered across the windshield; he was basically driving blind. Rolling down his window, he stuck his head out like a dog just to avoid running into a tree or another house. He tried the wiper fluid, but it was dry. Upon reaching the highway, he drove for a few more minutes, then stopped. Getting out of the truck, he began unbuttoning his uniform shirt, and after removing it, he revealed a black undershirt.

"Why are we stopping?" Kelly asked. Her voice was thick with panic.

John ignored her question and proceeded to wipe the blood off the windshield with his shirt. It wasn't working as well as he'd hoped, the shirt smearing the red blood across the windshield, making it even more difficult to see. He threw the shirt on the hood of the truck in frustration and grabbed the beer he'd taken for the road. He took one heavy swig before dumping the entire contents onto the windshield. The liquid foamed as it made contact with the blood-stained glass, but it worked. He wiped the windshield as clean as possible.

Kelly was now in full panic mode, her eyes wide in fear.

"John, why are we stopping?" she asked again. Mike held her close.

"Come on, John, let's get going," Mike said, becoming annoyed as John continued to wipe the glass.

"I can't see," John replied angrily. "You want me to drive into a tree or something?"

"Come on, Kelly, let's get in front with John," Mike said and climbed out of the rear bed and onto the pavement.

He helped Kelly down and the two climbed into the cab; Kelly sat in the middle and Mike was on her right. A few seconds later, John joined them.

John turned on the wipers to try and clear a little more of the blood off the windshield. It didn't help much so he stopped.

Still, it was a hundred times better than before, and now, at least he could see. He put the transmission into drive and began to drive, and in silence, the three made their way to Historic Downtown Cypress Pass.

32

Looking at her watch, Samantha saw that they'd been trapped for over four hours. For over an hour now it had been quiet, the banging on the walk-in door having ceased.

"Let's give it another half hour. If we don't hear anything, I'm opening the door to see if it's safe," Samantha said.

Simone didn't agree with her idea, but she was too tired to argue.

They waited another thirty minutes, and with silence still reigning, Samantha went to the door and opened it slowly, her hand on the handle in case she needed to close it quickly.

She poked her head out just enough to see. Nothing was there to greet her. The lights of the diner were still on and she crept low to the floor so she wouldn't be spotted, Simone staying in the walk-in for now.

Walking on all fours like a dog, she went behind the dining counter. Scattered in front of her were broken dishes, scattered silverware, and one badly-chewed arm laying in a thick puddle of blood. She placed her hand over her mouth and fought the feeling of nausea sweeping over her. She listened for any sounds before continuing but could only hear her own heavy breathing. Crawling to the glass refrigeration case, she took a few bottles of water from it, then cracked one open and drank from it.

"Simone!" she whispered with authority.

Simone poked her head out of the walk-in and Samantha rolled a bottle of water to her. She grabbed it and retreated back into her hiding place.

Samantha slowly rose up behind the counter and peered into the dining area. Tables were overturned, as were the chairs that accompanied them. Pools of blood and various bits of gore were splashed across the white tile floor like a bloody Picasso. Three of the six large windows facing the street were shattered and the glass door to the diner was barely hanging on its hinges. What was beyond the door caused her heart to drop.

The world outside of the diner was one of panic and chaos. In the dusky sky, she could make out plumes of dark smoke rising from various buildings.

People were running in what appeared to be a panic from other people who were methodically shuffling after them. She studied the shufflers and noticed that parts of their flesh had been torn from the bone. She was no doctor, but she was sure more than one of them had a broken leg or arm.

As she stared in shock, her mouth agape without her even realizing it, she saw Mr. Guillot, the owner of the bookstore, unload a pistol into the chest of one of the attackers—a man—who led others behind him. To her amazement, the man didn't fall, but continued onward.

She watched in horror as the man, who had a thin frame and a bald head, grabbed Mr. Guillot in his grasp and fell on top of him. Both men crashed to the ground and Mr. Guillot continued to fire his pistol wildly into the air. The rest of the group surrounded him and seemed to feed off his body like wild animals. The lead man tore into Mr. Guillot and tugged on his soft flesh and ropey sinew. Samantha felt the sudden, awful urge to vomit. She closed her eyes tightly and took a few deep breaths to help the feeling of nausea pass. She watched as the lead man stood up and walked toward a woman, who was getting into her car. In Samantha's mind she thought of these people as zombies from some of the horror movies she'd seen as a child. They sure acted the same. These people were maniacal killing machines that appeared to be focused only on death.

As the woman attempted to get into her car and escape, a group of zombies were on her before she could close the driver's door. Her screams quickly turned to wet gurgles and then nothing as her head was torn from her shoulders.

Samantha spotted Troy Sino, the local mechanic, standing in the middle of the street between the diner and the police station. Troy was a large man standing over six feet with a pot belly and a shaved head.

He was wielding a three foot long pipe-wrench and the muscles in his tattooed arms pulsed with each swing. He connected with the head of a woman in her thirties, and as the woman fell,

Troy stood over her and smashed her head repeatedly, blood and brain matter spraying from the tip of the wrench. Caught up in his rage, he didn't notice the group of four zombies behind him. They tackled him to the ground and in moments were tearing large pieces of soft flesh from his neck, back, and arms. He struggled and screamed but soon fell silent. The group continued to feed.

The street resembled a war zone, and as she continued to watch, tears ran down her face.

Her gaze went to the shutters on the sides of the window, then she saw the rolled-up security gate above the front door. If she could get everything closed, she and Simone would be safe.

She crawled to the first window on the far left of the diner. Silently rising, she reached up and closed the shutters, latching them in place. She was able to close the next two windows with ease. Reaching the front door, she looked up and saw the gate's handles. All she had to do was pull it down and lock it in place. As she crawled forward, her hand struck a rubbery piece of intestine. Her arm slipped out from under her and she went crashing to the floor with a thud.

Her chin smacked the cold tile and immediately the taste of blood filled her mouth. Shaking off the pain, she leapt to her feet and grabbed the handles of the gate. The zombies that were having a picnic over Troy heard the noise of the gate being moved and whipped around. They all started moving toward her as Samantha became visible in the doorway.

She grabbed the gate and pulled down hard. It didn't move. She tried again, this time clenching her teeth and letting out an animalistic roar, as she pulled down on it. Still nothing. She saw the zombies were closer, and when the first one was only a few feet away, she gave up on the gate and ran.

Soon, all the zombies had entered the diner as Samantha retreated back into the walk-in. She pulled it closed and she and

Simone huddled against the back wall, their eyes locked on the door, their breathing heavy in fear.

"I knew it was a bad idea to leave here," Simone said as tears welled up in her eyes.

Samantha didn't say anything, only sucked in a deep breath and tried not to cry, though she knew she was barely controlling herself. She was so scared it hurt.

Suddenly, the sound of multiple hands slapping the door echoed throughout the walk-in. The two women screamed with each blow, their bodies tense.

Hugging each other tightly, they cried together as the relentless sounds of the walking dead drowned them out.

33

An awkward silence filled the cab of the truck as the Ford inched closer to downtown. John had his eyes locked on the road, both hands never leaving the wheel. Mike was staring out the window into the swamp, the pistol in his hand ready for action. Kelly sat between them, her head resting on Mike's shoulder. In the distance, the sun was almost completely down, the darkness growing with each passing minute. Mike took a stab at breaking the silence.

"You really think it's a good idea to go downtown?"

"I do," John replied. "We need to get to the police station and check in."

"And why exactly do we need to get to the station?"

"Because I need to find out what the hell is going on around here," John said, his anger growing. He was the sheriff dammit and he didn't like to be second guessed.

"Listen, John, we don't know what's going on or if it's even possible to get to the station. What if we get downtown and those people are everywhere? The area won't be as spread out as it is now, we could get trapped in an alley or something. It could be suicide."

"Last time I remembered, we took an oath to protect the people of this town," John said.

An inner voice in his head suddenly shouted at him as the image of a running woman popped into his mind. *Just like you helped that woman, John? You're so full of shit!* He shook his head and the voice stopped.

"Look, Mike, I need all my officers on this and we need to figure out how to deal with this problem."

Mike gritted his teeth. "The only person I'm obligated to protect is Kelly. John, so let's just get out of here. Let the Army or the National Guard deal with it."

"We're going to the station, dammit," John said, his eyes creasing.

"Did you see how many of those people were at my house? Just think about it, damn it! You'll get us all killed!"

"Sorry, Mike, but my mind is made up."

Kelly sat up taller in her seat. After listening to the conversation in silence, John's bullheadedness finally made her add her point of view "And what if we don't *want* to go to the police station, John?" she asked, causing Mike to look at her.

There was only silence. John stared forward, concentrating on driving, as Kelly and Mike stared at him, waiting for an answer.

"John…" Mike finally said.

"You know what?" John said angrily as his foot slammed on the brake. The wheels screamed and squealed as the Ford came to a rest in the middle of the highway. "This is my fucking truck! I found it! And I came to get you both because I thought I could rely on you for help! If you don't want to come with me, then feel free to get the fuck out and walk! I'm going to the station!" when he finished, his finger pressed the automatic lock button.

The door locks shot up with a thunderous crack in the now silent cab. Kelly was too stunned to say anything. Her lip was trembling and it looked like she was going to cry at any moment. Mike looked into the side mirror and saw shadows dancing across the highway as the sun finished its descent. He wasn't sure if the shadows were from the setting sun or if there were more of those people now hunting them.

"Just drive, John," Mike said, his voice filled with defeat and aggravation. Mike knew it was a bad move going into town, but getting out and going it on foot would also be a mistake.

John removed his foot from the brake pedal and the Ford began to move forward, slowly picking up speed.

"I'm going to the police station," John repeated softly. "All of us are."

"We sure the hell are," Mike replied with a sigh.

Kelly said nothing; the tears rolling down her face said it all.

34

In only half a day, the small town of Cypress Pass had come to resemble a Third World country. As the Ford truck entered downtown, the scenery had changed dramatically from earlier that day.

Many of the small business were now engulfed in flames. Bodies littered the street. Some with bullet holes in their heads, others with body parts chewed away. A car had caught fire and exploded against the small book and music store, causing the quaint building to collapse. People were still running in the street, but the number of people perusing them was greater and the runners now fewer. The police station had remained virtually untouched throughout the chaos. Its heavy fortified doors and elevated windows made it a difficult building to access.

Meanwhile, Samantha and Simone were still trapped inside the walk-in, as the growing numbers of living dead banged and clawed at the metal door separating them from an easy meal. Surrounding the chaos, the crickets chirped, the frogs croaked, and the fireflies danced, oblivious to the town's destruction.

35

Eighteen-year-old Eddy Dunlop was not doing well. His short, plump frame was pressed against the make-shift barricade in the conference room of the police station. He nervously ran his fingers through his black, spiky hair as his chest rose and fell rapidly with each heavy breath. His hands were gripped tightly around a wooden baseball bat so tight that his knuckles flashed a pale white. His eyes darted back and forth in the room as the sounds from outside startled him. Suddenly, the bright beam of a flashlight struck him in the face. He let out a startled cry and shielded his eyes from the painful glare.

"Turn that damn light off!" a voice ordered.

Mayor Dunlop was sitting across the room from his son, fidgeting with the flashlight he'd found a few minutes ago in a desk.

"Son, don't tell me what to do. Can't you see I'm trying save our lives," Dunlop responded.

Roger Gentrie took a step forward. The glow of the moonlight through the windows accented the tight muscles in his arms and the contours of his face. He worked in one of the chemical refineries as a laborer in the next town over, but his looks could have had him working as an actor in Hollywood or as a model. His long, brown hair fell around his neck as he walked over to the mayor.

"No dipshit, you're going to get us killed, now keep that light out."

"Do you know who you're talking to, *boy*?" Dunlop asked, growing angry.

"A dead old man if you don't give me that damn flashlight," Roger replied.

Dunlop was stunned by the attitude of the young punk, but before he could say anything more, Roger reached out and snatched the flashlight from Dunlop's loose grip. For a moment, it looked like he might retaliate, but instead he just sat back against the wall he was leaning against.

"I'll remember that when this is all over. Believe you me," Dunlop said menacingly.

"Guys, please, just calm down," June Dunlop said.

She'd been crouched underneath the conference room table. She had a pretty face that would have been made prettier with a little makeup. From playing housewife all her life, she had grown chubby, and her black hair was pulled back in a messy pony tail.

"Damn it, June, just stay out of this and shut the hell up," Dunlop yelled at his wife.

June recoiled back under the table. Although she'd stopped loving her husband years ago, the pain of his words always cut her deep.

"Fuckin' asshole," Roger hissed as he switched the flashlight off and stormed away. He walked across the room to where June was hiding and he crouched down so his face was even with hers. "In case you get scared," he said and handed her the flashlight, showing her a smile as bright as the light.

"Thank you," she whispered as her hand grazed his.

The moonlight streaming in from the windows made June look stunning to Roger, and he could feel the wanting of her taking hold. They'd been sleeping together for a few months now, ever since Roger started hanging around Eddy. One day he'd swung by the house to see if Eddy was home but had just missed him. June invited him in for something to drink and it didn't take long before she was crying on his shoulder about her shallow marriage and her meaningless life.

She had been drinking of course, as her new routine was to start the day with a few screwdrivers, light on the OJ, and the feeling of Roger holding her in his strong arms had excited her. She'd lured him into the bedroom she shared with the person she had come to despise and loved every moment as Roger ravaged her on the side of the bed Dunlop slept on.

Roger was young, strong, and willing to do anything. And he loved it when a portrait of Mayor Dunlop was looking down at him as he gave it to his old lady.

Oblivious to the affair, Dunlop wondered why someone like Roger would even want to hang around with his dumbass son, and Roger got a kick out of him not knowing what was going on behind closed doors. At the moment, June was tempted to yank Roger under the table with her, but he broke the tension.

"Everything's cool. We're safe up here," he reassured her and she believed him, though it was hard to feel safe when she looked at the crudely constructed barricade.

Behind Roger were the double doors to the conference room. In front of it was a jumbled pile of chairs, a desk, and a large book-shelf. The doors of the conference room had been made of solid wood as well, but Dunlop insisted they barricade themselves in.

Standing up, Eddy paced in front the barricade. Every now and then, he would shake a chair or reach through the furniture and touch the doors. "I don't think it's going to hold for long," he said, clutching the bat tighter as he stepped back, almost like he expected to be attacked that very moment. "We're gonna die up here, I know it!" His voice was louder, his eyes wide with fright;

sweat beaded on his forehead. He wasn't far from having a break-down.

"Eddy, just take it easy, buddy," Roger said, trying to calm Eddy down. Unfortunately, it wasn't working.

"We never should have come up here! We're trapped! Trapped!"

"Eddy, shut the fuck up!" Roger yelled back. "No one's going to die."

But Eddy wasn't convinced. He let out a long sigh as he placed his back against the wall and slid down heavily to the floor. He slowly rocked back and forth as he wept quietly into his shirt.

Mayor Dunlop shook his head with disgust at the pussy he sadly called a son. He stood up and walked over to a window which overlooked the street and saw ten to fifteen zombies walk-ing the street, eagerly searching for their next meal. He observed several packs that were crouched on the ground, making a feast of some poor soul. His heart dropped as he watched the town he helped grow burn and crumple in front of him. He didn't give a shit about the redneck idiots that called Cypress Pass home, but the town was his legacy...and his legacy was dying.

Pulling him from his reverie, two dim beams of light caught his attention as he gazed out the window. Though they were off in the distance, he could tell they were headlights and were coming his way. Dunlop could actually feel himself getting excited. Soon, the vehicle would pull up and the zombies would attack the poor fools inside. He was looking forward to a show, something to at least entertain him while he was trapped.

He figured he might as well tell the others, and the news would shut Eddy up about how safe they were. Turning to face the others, he said, "Someone's coming," with little-to-no emotion.

The others all looked up in surprise, their eyes wide as they filled with hope. Was it someone coming to rescue them? Roger leapt from where he was sitting and ran to the window.

"What is it?" June asked.

"Looks like a pickup truck," Roger said, his face pressed against the cool glass. His hot breath fogged the window slightly. He glanced back at Eddy.

"Can you grab the flashlight for me? I'm gonna see if I can signal them."

As soon as he finished his sentence, Dunlop was on him. With a hard shove, he pushed Roger away from the window. Roger went crashing to the floor and slid a few feet.

"You'll do no such a thing! They'll bring those things right to us! Thank the good Lord you're nothing but a field hand, 'cause you don't have shit for brains, boy," Dunlop snapped.

Roger was on his feet in an instant. He flew at Dunlop and grabbed the older man's shirt collar with his calloused hands. He wanted to beat the hell out of Dunlop, but somehow found the ability to restrain himself. Instead, he shoved Dunlop hard against the window the mayor was just looking out of.

"They could have guns! They could get us out of here! What if it's the military coming in to do a search and rescue or something? We have to let them know we're in here!" Roger said.

"They could also be sick with whatever the rest of the town has. If we let them in and they're crazy too, they'll attack us. It's not gonna happen, boy, not with my family in here."

What Dunlop meant to say was not with *himself* in here. Roger could feel his right hand balling into a tight fist, but before he could raise it to strike, June was there, standing between them.

"He's right, Roger. If they're infected, they could turn on us."

Roger stared at her in disbelief, his heart feeling like it had been ripped in two. Thoughts rushed into his mind: *She sided with him? Did I just hear that? After all she's told me about how she hated him?* He felt as if the wind had been knocked out of him, and the sight of Dunlop's smug face with his obnoxious rooster beak made him so angry it took every ounce of his will not to explode and beat the mayor into a bloody mess.

"Fine. Do whatever the fuck you want. With Mayor Shithead running the show, we'll either be dead soon or will probably be joining those bastards trying to kill us."

Dunlop, June, and Roger were so busy arguing that they'd stopped looking out the window to see what the approaching vehicle was actually doing.

Standing up once more, Eddy had gathered what courage he had left and went to look at the approaching vehicle.

"It looks like they're coming here," Eddy said, his voice cracking.

The other three looked out the window to see the unfolding spectacle as the truck got closer.

Finally, something interesting, Dunlop thought, a small smile creeping across his sweaty face.

36

"So, do you have a plan, John?" Mike asked as the smoking town drew closer.

"Sort of."

"Sort of?" Kelly yelled. "What's your plan, John?"

"Well, I figured I'd get us as close to the front door to the station as I can. When I pull up, you and Mike jump out and get the door open. I'll cover y'all. Once we get inside, we should be all right. The doors are made of heavy oak and there's no way someone can break through them without tools, let alone people that are actually dead. Also, the windows are seven feet off the ground, and if you remember how those things acted at your house, they don't seem to be able to climb very well if at all."

"They don't seem to have any intelligence, either. When Kelly and I were on the roof, they just stared up at us and moaned. They couldn't figure out how to get to us," Mike added.

"Exactly," John said. "They also don't appear to be very fast. They seem to move at a speed walk, but they're horribly uncoordinated. If we keep our heads and everyone does what they need to do, we'll be inside the station and safe in no time."

"And then what?" Kelly asked, not convinced.

"Then we can stay put until help arrives. We have weapons in the armory, some food in the break room, water from the water cooler, and radios and phones to contact someone. We'll be safe. And if we need to, we can also go upstairs to the conference room and secure it. That room also has heavy doors like the front entrance."

Kelly was surprisingly pleased with John's explanation.

"Sounds like a solid idea to me," Mike agreed.

"Good, because we're almost there."

The F-150 clipped the side of the wooden sign proclaiming their arrival into Historical Downtown Cypress Pass. The old sign shattered into splinters as it fell to the ground. John smiled a little, even though he hadn't meant to hit it, but at the same time the irony of the words struck him as funny. Downtown Cypress Pass was indeed a thing of history. Before him stood a hollowed out shell of the town he knew. It reminded him of a carved pumpkin that was once so proud but was now a sagging, rotting mess.

Kelly gasped as the Ford's driver side mirror struck the head of a small zombie boy and sent him rolling off the side. The mirror disappeared upon impact. Mike was busy counting the undead in the street. He stopped counting when he was over thirty.

"Stay calm and we'll get through this," John said as he ran down three bodies and then hit a fourth with the corner of the front bumper. The zombie fell to the ground with a broken hip and began to crawl after the vehicle. The truck bounced up and down spastically as it encountered numerous zombie speed bumps.

John's eyes were fixed on the upcoming police station. On the cement walk in front of it, a small group of zombies had gathered, hungrily gazing up at the second floor window.

He glanced at the diner for a moment and his heart sank when he saw the smashed windows and broken door. *So much for meeting someone new,* he thought.

They were less than a hundred feet from the police station and John's heart was pounding with anticipation. "The second I stop, you two get that door open. I'll cover you. We clear?"

Kelly and Mike both nodded.

"Then let's do this!" he yelled as the F-150 smashed into the group of zombie gawkers.

Bits of bone, organs, and appendages flew into the air followed by a fountain of congealed blood and other bodily fluids.

The truck stopped and its tires gave a loud screech as dirt and grass were thrown up into the air.

Jumping out of the vehicle, Mike had the key to the front door in his hand and Kelly was close behind him with her gun drawn as they rounded the truck and headed up the stairs to the Cypress Pass Police Station.

John grabbed his rifle and stood behind the bed of the truck, glancing over his shoulder every few seconds, not wanting to be taken by surprise.

The mob of zombies on the street saw the meal in front of them and turned as one group to go after them. As they quickly lurched toward John, he took aim. He was careful and calm with his shots, and with each pull of the trigger, a zombie hit the ground with half its head gone, never to move again. He continually checked his sides to make sure he wasn't about to be ambushed, a chill running down his spine in anticipation of an attack.

For just a second, he realized he was enjoying himself, despite the horrifying situation of having to shoot people down like wild dogs. But he knew these weren't innocent people, they were monsters that wanted to kill him.

Mike and Kelly were not enjoying themselves. The key fit inside the lock perfectly, but when Mike went to push the door open, he found it wouldn't budge. He put his shoulder into it hard but it barely moved.

"What's wrong?" Kelly asked, panicking.

"The door won't open. I think there's something in the way," he grunted and slammed his shoulder into the door. It only moved an inch.

"Guys, what's taking so long?" John yelled and took down another walking corpse. When the body hit the ground, what was left of its brain spilled out to splash the pavement.

"There's something in front of the door! It won't move!" Mike called back.

"Shit," John muttered. "Mike, I'm almost out of ammo. I need your help!"

"Goddamn it!" Mike shouted. "Kelly, I need to help John or we're all gonna die. Try to get this door open!"

Mike lowered his shoulder and ran into it three more times. Each time the door was pushed open a little more. He then turned and ran to John, his gun already drawn.

Kelly began kicking the door with everything she had and could feel the door opening just a little more each time.

John's rifle clicked empty after he put down his seventieth zombie. He pulled his 9mm but he had to wait for them to get closer so he could make an accurate shot.

Mike ran next to him and fired twice, but his bullets harmlessly lodged into a zombie's shoulder and another in a stomach.

John fired his last bullet. "I'm dry. Give me yours and load mine!" he ordered and Mike took the pistol and handed John the .40. Mike grabbed a fresh 9mm clip from John's belt.

John looked up and fired. For every zombie he put down, another two seemed to take its place.

It was only a matter of time before they would be overrun. Looking over his shoulder, he saw more coming their way.

"Kelly, how's that door coming?" Mike yelled.

"Almost got it!" she replied. Two zombies began walking toward her and she turned and shot each one, sending them sprawling back to the ground. She spun back around and began working on the door again.

John handed the empty .40 to Mike who gave him back the loaded pistol. John stared at the oncoming zombie horde, took aim, and started firing.

37

Samantha and Simone perked up when a faint popping sound, barely audible, could be heard through the metal doors of the walk-in.

"It sounds like someone's making popcorn," Simone said, puzzled.

Samantha placed a finger to her lips and motioned for Simone to be quiet. The pounding on the doors had ceased the moment the popping sounds were heard.

Samantha even heard the sound of a dozen feet shuffling away, like children whose interest was captivated by a new toy. Curiosity was getting the better of her and she debated opening the door, but it finally took hold of her and she walked over to the metal door, unlocked it, and gripped the handle.

"What are you doing?" Simone gasped, rising to her feet so quickly it surprised Samantha.

"I think they're gone, and I want to find out what made them leave," she said.

"But they're out there, don't open it, please."

Samantha would have none of it. "Look, I'll be careful," she said and cracked the door an inch.

The opening was just enough for her to peer through, and she saw nothing but the darkness of a destroyed diner. She breathed a sigh of relief and gave a thumbs up to Simone, who only shook her head and crossed her arms, not wanting to venture out of the safety of the walk-in. Samantha opened the door a little more and squeezed her thin frame through the opening.

She could hear the popping again, and this time she knew exactly what it was—gunfire. She cautiously walked to one of the still open windows to look onto the street.

A group of zombies was quickly making their way to the police station. Every few seconds, one would drop and the others would press on, totally oblivious that they'd lost one of their own.

On the steps of the station she saw one man shooting and the other holding a gun. Above them, a woman was kicking viciously at the door.

The man shooting had his arm up, blocking his face, but when he lowered it, Samantha's eyes grew wide and she smiled.

"Simone! It's John!" she yelled and dashed back to Simone, who was still pouting.

The sudden return of Samantha almost caused Simone to pass out in fear and she could have sworn she felt the twinge of a heart attack. Thankfully, the pain in her arm faded as fast as it arrived.

"Come on, Simone, we have to get out of here!"

"I'm not going anywhere. We're safe here and an old lady like me can't be running around dodging crazy people."

"Please, Simone, come with me. We'll be safer with John in the police station. He'll have a plan to get us to safety."

"No, dear, I'm not going anywhere. I'll just stay in here, thank you very much." She crossed her arms and looked away, the matter settled.

Samantha could hear the gunfire as the battle raged on outside. She looked at the exit to the diner, then back to Simone.

"Well, I'm not staying here. I'll send help for you once I get away, I promise."

"Good luck, dear, my prayers are with you," Simone said.

Samantha nodded, turned, and left. Simone looked at the slightly open door and her heart began to race.

She was alone and could feel the loneliness swirling around her, the room quickly becoming very small to her senses. Simone knew she was on the verge of a panic attack. Suddenly she decided being alone was far worse than what waited for her outside.

"Samantha, wait for me!" she shouted.

Standing up, she began to waddle out of the broken walk-in as fast as her legs would allow.

38

"Switch!" John yelled and Mike quickly placed his loaded gun into John's open hand.

"Kelly, how's it coming?" Mike called out.

"Almost got it!" she replied while delivering kick after kick to the heavy door.

She took a few steps back and ran forward, delivering a thunderous kick that sent one of the chairs blocking the door tumbling. The space was tight, but she was able to squeeze through. She climbed over a desk and began throwing furniture off it. After it was clear, she gathered all her strength and pushed the heavy desk out of the way. The veins in her arms and forehead were pulsing and she let out an animalistic howl deep from within her as she cleared the door.

"Come on!" she screamed.

Mike turned and saw the open door.

"Come on, John, time to go!"

John took one more shot and dropped a large man with a thick black beard and a trucker hat. Just as John made it up the first step, a voice from the undead crowd called out to him.

"John!" It was a woman's voice.

He looked around, startled, amazed that these dead people could even talk. He stared out into the sea of dead, moaning faces.

Then he saw her. She was still wearing her waitress uniform from earlier as she ran toward him.

"Samantha!" he yelled in excitement and left the step to begin making his way to her.

Mike had reached the front door, and when he turned around, he was shocked that John wasn't behind him. He saw John heading into the street, dodging zombies as he cut a jagged course.

"John! What the hell are you doing?"

"Just cover me for a minute!" he yelled back.

John ran toward Samantha with his pistol drawn. Just as he'd thought, the creatures were off balanced and easy to maneuver around.

When he reached her, they embraced in a quick hug for second before he grabbed her hand and began dragging her to the police station.

"Wait, John! Simone's still in the diner. We have to go get her!"

John turned to tell her that wasn't happening, but then he saw Simone running out of the diner toward them.

"Please wait, don't leave me!" Simone screamed as she waddle-jogged to them.

A dead teenage girl with matted brown hair and a tube top, quickly pursued the slow moving older woman. John sent a bullet whizzing by Simone and the girl dropped with a large hole in her head.

As she fell, her hand reached out and her jagged fingernails dug into the soft flesh of Simone's calf. Simone didn't notice as the blood poured from the wound and down her leg.

Samantha grabbed Simone's hand and the two women ran to the police station. John lingered behind them, keeping any zombie who tried to attack them at bay with a well-placed shot to the head.

The three quickly made their way up the stairs, where Mike was motioning them on like a third base coach telling the runner to steal home plate.

They all ran inside and Mike slammed the door, then locked it and began piling furniture against it. Within moments, they could hear the thud of fists pounding on the other side.

"They'll never get through," Mike said reassuringly.

The old oak doors were a half inch thick with large iron dead bolts. The police station was elevated six and a half feet off the ground, and the large windows which ran down the front hall were out of reach for the outstretched hands of the walking dead.

"Is everyone all right?" John asked after the weary survivors had caught their breath.

"I got cut on my leg somehow, but otherwise I'm fine," Simone said with a whimper.

John knelt down and almost gasped when he saw the wound. It was on the back of Simone's calf and was caked with blood. An inch of loose flesh hung from the hole.

A small piece of chipped fingernail was still embedded in the skin around it, informing him of how Simone had been injured. It already looked infected.

"There's a first aid kit in my secretary's office. I'll be right back," John said and began to walk away.

"Wait up for a second, will ya?" Mike called.

"What is it?"

"The doors were barricaded from the inside. Someone's in here and we don't know if they're like us or like the ones outside. I'm coming with you."

"No, Mike. If that's the case then I need you to stay here and protect the others. I'll be fine. I'm just going down the hall. Trust me, if I need help you'll hear me."

"All right, fine. Just be careful."

John turned and made his way down the dark hall. He was cautious as he passed each doorway, making sure nothing was inside, waiting to surprise him. He only had to walk about fifty feet before coming to Diane's office.

He entered and jumped back in surprise when he saw her. She was lying slumped against the wall. Her head had been smashed in so badly that he couldn't see her face anymore.

But he recognized the color of her hair and the shape of her body, there was no doubt that the corpse was Diane, his secretary.

"Oh, Diane, no," he whispered kneeling down beside her.

He touched her hand lightly and felt the cold, dead flesh. *I hope you're with your husband*, he thought. He stood up and removed the first aid kit from the wall. On his way out, he closed the door to the office and headed back to the others.

"You see anyone?" Mike asked.

"Yeah. Diane's dead," John said as he shook his head.

"Son-of-a-bitch," Mike whispered.

John used a few pads of rubbing alcohol to clean Simone's wound, then removed the fingernail with a pair of plastic tweezers.

When Simone grew nervous, he said it was a rock so she wouldn't panic. A spray of antiseptic medication caused her to wince. With the wound clean, he pressed some clean gauze to it and wrapped it with an Ace bandage.

"Good as new," he said with a grin.

She smiled back and Samantha helped Simone off the chair she was sitting on.

"We should go upstairs and see if anyone's in here," Mike said. "Actually, there really is no *if* about it. Someone put all that stuff in front of the door so they have to still be in this building."

"Could be one of the other deputies?" John suggested. "Maybe they're upstairs."

"I don't know. A deputy would've known there was no point in barricading those doors. That they were heavy enough to take anything thrown at them."

"Well, we need to get some more guns before we start searching. We're running pretty low on ammo, too," John said.

He took his half-empty pistol and handed it to Samantha.

"Easy stuff. Just point and shoot," he said. She took the gun with a bit of hesitation.

"Let me see your gun, Kelly," Mike said as she handed it to him.

He reloaded it with the few bullets he had left in his pocket and returned it to her. He turned to look at Simone. "Can you shoot?"

"Oh Lord no," she said with her arms up in protest, "I'll be more likely to shoot myself in the leg before shooting one of those things."

"Everyone gets a gun, Simone," John said as he searched through the desks of his officers. "Just don't put your finger on the trigger till you need to and only aim it at someone you intend to shoot. You'll be fine." He went to a third desk and opened the top drawer, where another pistol was inside.

One of his deputies hadn't taken it with him when leaving the station. This happened often, as Cypress Pass was usually a quiet town and his men had become complacent. He'd chided his men constantly about it, but now it was fortunate.

Simone reluctantly took the gun after John made sure it was loaded and the safety was off. She held it like it was a dead fish.

"What about y'all?" Samantha asked.

"We're covered," John said and walked down the hall.

The group followed behind him closely as he came to the second door on his right. He removed his keys and opened the door, which lead to another door, this one metal, with a lock combination.

He placed his key inside the key hole and turned the lock to the appropriate numeric pattern. The sound of the lock disengaging was loud in the silent hallway.

He swung the door open, slid a metal gate to the side, and strolled into the Cypress Pass Police Armory.

He flipped on the light switch and the fluorescent bulbs overhead illuminated the room. Shotguns, pistols, and flare guns lined the shelves. A few old SWAT suits hung on metal hangers with the helmets perched above them.

Straight ahead at the end of the room was a shelf stacked with boxes of ammunition.

John removed a Remington 870 police pump action shotgun from the wall and loaded it with five shells, then attached a tactical flashlight to it before handing it to Mike, who removed a 9mm pistol and began stocking up on ammunition.

He loaded three more of the pistols and handed one to each of the women.

John removed another shotgun from the wall, loaded it, and attached a flashlight to it. He removed a .40 and holstered it.

He loaded his police belt with as much ammunition as it could carry.

"What about the SWAT suits?" Mike asked and picked up a helmet. "They could come in handy if we get into any close contact with a zombie."

Kelly blinked and said, "Did you really just say the word zombies, Mike? Seriously?"

"Well yeah, they're dead and they're trying to kill us; seems the most appropriate word, don't ya think?"

"Mike, don't call them zombies," John said. "And have you ever worn one of those suits? I doubt your big ass would even fit in one. Dunlop picked them up from some police auction because he wanted Cypress Pass to have them. Damn things are tight as hell and almost impossible to move in."

Mike shrugged and returned the helmet to its place on the shelf. He thought he would have looked cool in it.

"Grab whatever else you need. Weapons, ammo, anything," John said as the group began stocking up.

After they'd made a sizeable dent in the inventory of the armory, they gathered in the hall to discuss their next move.

"Here's what we'll do," John said. "We'll go up the stairs to the second floor. There's a conference room there with a small bathroom. I say we hole up in there for a while. The doors are big and heavy, like the doors on the first floor. We'll also have enough room to spread out, and there are windows that we can look out of as well."

No one disagreed with the plan and the group of five made a single file line: John in front, followed by Samantha, Simone, Kelly, and Mike protecting the rear.

They walked up the short stairwell and entered a hall lined with cold, white tiles.

"The conference room is the door at the very end of the hall," Mike said to the women, who nodded their heads when they saw the large, brown double doors.

They passed a small office, two interrogation rooms, and a bathroom before making it to the double doors of the conference room.

John placed his hand on the door handle and pushed.

The door didn't even budge.

39

Dunlop, Roger, and Eddy still had their faces pressed against the windows, looking out on the street.

A growing mass of zombies were collecting at the entrance to the police station.

Dunlop could see the ones in the front of the line being crushed with the weight of their brethren as the mob pressed forward.

They had all witnessed the group of people fighting their way inside the station, but had since lost sight of them.

However, they knew they had gotten inside, and the thought chilled Dunlop to the bone.

Suddenly, the sound of a muffled cry and the slight thump on the double doors made them jump, then more muffled cursing could be heard coming from behind the barricade.

"We have to open it," Eddy said and made his way to the doors.

"You won't do a damn thing!" Dunlop ordered. "They'll let all those things in here and then we can kiss our asses goodbye. 'Prob'ly why they want to get in here in the first place. Got them things high on their asses."

"But we can't just leave them out there! It's murder!" Eddy pleaded with his stubborn father, knowing he was fighting a battle he would never win.

"Eddy, your father is right," June said.

"See? It's either us or them, boy! Think of your family! You got as much sense as a goddamn catfish! Must have gotten that from your mother's side."

Roger had heard enough. He was already on the edge of exploding since June had sided with Dunlop. Now this attack on her drove him over the edge.

I'll show her what I can do. What a man can do, he thought and rushed toward Dunlop. Before the mayor could react, Roger was on him. With a hard shove, Dunlop fell to the floor and slid across it. He stared up at Roger in disbelief. No one had ever treated him like that before.

"Look around, asshole! You aren't in charge of shit anymore! You don't run this conference room and you sure as hell ain't the mayor of zombieville!" Roger screamed, his face turning bright red.

Roger went over to the barricade and started removing the stacks of furniture.

June had her hand over her heart and could feel it thumping in her chest. She was so turned on by Roger's animalistic outburst.

"Help me out, Eddy," Roger ordered as he struggled to move a desk.

Eddy joined him and together they pushed the large wooden desk out of the way.

"You idiots! You're going to get us killed!" Dunlop yelled, still on the floor.

"Dad, shut up for once, please," Eddy said as the barricade came down piece by piece.

40

In a small clearing approximately ten miles away from the police station, deep inside the swamp, two helicopters were preparing for departure.

The four pilots, two to an aircraft, sat in their cockpits and began flipping switches. The control panel glowed neon green in the dark night. As they moved more switches, the rotors began to spin as the engines cycled.

"Vegas Six-Two-Six, this is Reno One, radio check. How do you hear?" said the pilot in the first helicopter.

"All good, Reno One."

The pilot clicked more switches and the helicopter came to life. The rotors began rapidly slicing through the humid air, causing small saplings to blow over and the surrounding swamp water to splash.

The anti-collision lights flashed a bright red glow, illuminating the area around them.

"Vegas Six-Two-Six, ground checks complete. Are we clear for go?" the same pilot said.

After Vegas confirmed they were, the rotor blades spun faster, the sound droning in the night.

The first helicopter slowly lifted off the ground and disappeared into the darkness, the second one following a second later.

41

As the doors to the conference room were opened, John, Samantha, Simone, Kelly, and Mike rushed in. Thinking he would be treated as a hero, Eddy was stunned when he found a shotgun pointed in his face.

"Get back!" John ordered, then switched his attention to Roger. "Both of you, on the wall, now!"

Eddy was afraid he was going to piss himself. He could feel his bladder already starting to loosen.

"John?" Mayor Dunlop said.

John turned and saw the mayor sitting on the floor. "Mayor?" he said, and rushed over to help Dunlop to his feet.

"Can we put our hands down now?" Eddy asked.

"Yes, son, it's all right," Dunlop said.

Eddy and Roger dropped their hands to their sides. Each let out a collective sigh of relief.

"John, you remember my family? My son Eddy and my wife June?"

John turned and received a slight wave from June.

"But I don't think you've met his dumbass friend, Roger," Dunlop said, pointing at him. "Unless you've arrested him."

Roger gave Dunlop a one finger salute.

"It's great you're here, John, and you too, Mike. Good to have some officers in here. You know, our pal Roger just pushed me to the floor. I believe that's assault. I don't think it benefits us to have a person here who would strike a public official. Do you?"

John looked over at Roger who had a stunned look on his face.

"What are you saying, Mayor?" Mike asked.

"Well, I think we should lock him up in one of the holding cells, is all. Keep him from harming us until this whole thing blows over," Dunlop said, a pleased grin smeared across his sweaty face.

"You have got to be kidding me," Roger said.

"Mayor, I'm sorry if you and the boy are having issues, but tensions are running high right now and frankly, I think we need all the people we can get. I'm not locking anyone up tonight," John replied.

A look of shock washed over Dunlop's once smiling face. It was quickly replaced with anger. "Now you listen here, Sheriff, and I use that term very loosely if you don't listen to what I tell you. You do as I say or you won't be the sheriff for much longer. Out of the police force, out of Cypress Pass, and out of this here conference room!"

"I think you need to calm down, Mayor," John said, his eyes locking with Dunlop's gaze. "Besides, in times of distress, the sheriff takes power to ensure all citizens are protected. And I think you'd agree that this is most definitely a time of distress."

"I don't give a shit what the rules are! I'm the mayor of this town and I'm ordering you to lock that punk up right now!"

The cocking of Mike's shotgun filled in the large room.

"I think you need to do what the sheriff says and calm down, Mayor," Mike said.

"This is mutiny! This is treason!" Dunlop stammered, shocked. He gazed around the room for some form of support. When it was clear no one cared what he had to say, he turned around angrily and sat down in the far corner of the room.

"Why were the downstairs front doors blocked?" John asked. "Those doors could have a car run into them and probably wouldn't budge."

"Sorry, we just panicked," Roger replied.

"How'd you all get here?" Kelly asked.

"Me and Roger were at my house playing Playstation when my dad came bursting into my room. He was yelling to get into the car. That something bad had happened. We all piled in and drove down here. I could see people running and getting tackled by other people. Mom was crying and Dad just kept speeding along. We got to the police station and pulled up around back. Dad parked behind the gated parking lot. He rushed us all inside and told us to start putting stuff in front of the front doors. Then Diane came out of her office. I waved hello to her but she didn't wave back. She just sort of stared at me like she wasn't looking at me, you know? Like she didn't recognize me. She let out this low moan that's still in my head. It was like the sound an owl makes before it swoops up a mouse, then she came at me. I dodged out of the way but she grabbed my shirt. I can still see her eyes and smell her bad breath, like death and rot all rolled into one. It was awful."

"How'd you get away?" Samantha asked.

"I found a bat in a closet and bashed her head in," Roger said proudly.

"You shut your fucking mouth, you little piece of shit," John growled, his eyes burning holes into Roger's now-pale face. "She was a good person and she didn't deserve to die like that."

"Keep going, Eddy. What happened next?" Mike said.

"Not really much else to say," Eddy shrugged. "We piled some furniture behind the front doors and came up here and locked ourselves in. Dad said it was the safest thing to do until the Army arrives."

John's attention turned to Dunlop, who was resting against his left shoulder, staring straight ahead, seeing nothing.

"I have a question, Mayor. How did you know to come here and get to safety while the rest of the town ran around like a bunch of headless chickens?"

"That information is private, Sheriff."

"Private my ass! How did you know to come here while everyone else was dying? Seems like you know exactly what's going on around here."

"Fuck off, John. I don't answer to you," Dunlop snapped.

John paused for a second, taking in the disrespectful words. Around him, the entire room was silent. "Mike, open the window," John said, pointing to the one next to the mayor.

Mike knew what was about to go down, and he was more than happy to oblige.

"What exactly do you think you're doing, Deputy?" Dunlop asked Mike, but John was already yanking him up by his shirt collar before he could finish the sentence.

Mike opened the window and a rush of cool air flooded the room. It carried with it the stench of smoke, death and blood.

"If you aren't going to help us, then you're of no use to us," John said and punched the mayor in the stomach.

Immediately Dunlop felt his knees buckle and the air rush out of his lungs. He felt Mike grab his shoulders and lean him back out the open window as John grabbed his legs. Outside, Dunlop could hear the excited moans of the living dead below him.

"Tell us what you know, Dunlop, or out you go!" John yelled.

"I told you, I can't!"

"Maybe you don't understand, Mayor. I'm going to drop you, and when I do, one of two things is going to happen. Either you're going to hit the lottery and fall right on your head, killing yourself instantly, or you're going to break your legs and back and have to wait for death to come while they eat you alive!"

"Stop, you don't understand!" Dunlop cried as tears ran down his face.

"Fine. Goodbye, Mayor!" John yelled as he began to push him out the window.

"No wait! I'll tell! I'll tell you everything! Don't drop me!"

"You promise," Mike asked.

"Yes! Please, pull me back in! For the love of God, I don't want to die!"

John and Mike pulled Dunlop back into the room where he crumpled to the floor. Neither June nor Eddy rushed to his side.

"Spill it," John ordered; he wasn't screwing around anymore.

"Colonel Dillon called me and told me that something bad was about to go down," Dunlop blubbered. "He didn't say terrorists but he was strongly implying it. He said some chemical had been released and it was reanimating corpses, turning them into mind-less killing machines. He told me to get my family and go some-place safe, that very soon all hell would be breaking loose. I gathered everyone up and came here. This was the only place I could think of. That's all I know! I swear!"

"You see, boss, I told you they were zombies," Mike said.

John was stunned. He had witnessed some horrible things in Iraq and Afghanistan, but the situation they were now in made him long to be in a bunker again.

"So, what are we going to do?" Eddy asked, directing his question to John.

"I really don't know right now," was all John could think to say.

"Well, we need to get out of here," Kelly said.

"And go where?" Samantha asked. "Because last time I checked, there were flesh-eating corpses out there and none in here."

"Does anyone have a better idea?" Kelly asked, disregarding Samantha's response, but no one answered.

John looked down at his cell phone. It still had **NO SERVICE** displayed across the small screen. "Anyone have a signal?" he asked.

Everyone checked their phones but the message was the same on all of them. Mike walked over to the phone in the middle of the conference room. He picked up the receiver and listened; it was silent.

"We tried that already," June said sheepishly.

Mike hung the phone up and sat in one of the hard metal chairs that lined the conference room table.

"We need to get to the next town," Simone said.

"I'm not going anywhere. We're safe in here," June replied.

"I don't really give a goddamn what y'all decide, but I'm not stepping foot out of this police station," Dunlop added.

"Why don't we just wait till morning," Roger suggested.

Roger looked at John, who shrugged his shoulders. It did sound like a good plan for now.

"It'll be much easier to navigate in the day than at night," Mike said.

"Yeah, and much easier for those things to see us," Eddy argued.

"Still, I'd rather be able to see where I'm running to," John said. "And I think we could all use some sleep."

The weary group all nodded at the thought of some sleep.

Outside, an eerie quiet had gripped the small town of Cypress Pass. In the distance, one last person gave a blood-curdling scream before falling silent; the snaps and cracks of burning wood from nearby buildings faded into the darkness.

"What if they get in while we're asleep?" Kelly asked. "What if those fires spread to this building?"

"This building is mostly brick, it won't catch fire," John said. "And we can take turns keeping watch for the night. Two people every two hours should be good enough. If you want, we can even reinforce the furniture against the front doors. The back door is made out of steel so that one should be good to go."

John and Mike headed downstairs. Soon, the sounds of heavy furniture being dragged across the floor mixed with the eerie silence filing the hallways.

Thirty minutes later, the two men returned to the conference room.

"I'll take first watch," John said. "Anyone want to go with me?"

"I'll do it," Eddy said.

"Good man," John replied. He cocked his shotgun and handed it to Eddy.

42

It wasn't long before sleep came to the worn-out group of survivors. Dunlop was silently snoring in his corner of the room. Samantha and Kelly were huddled next to one another under the conference table with June.

Roger was sitting in a chair, his head nestled in his arms on the conference table. Mike was lying on top of the table. Simone had her back against the wall furthest from the doors.

Unknown to everyone, her heart had failed within a few moments of her being asleep and the surreal sensation of death had washed her away from the nightmare she'd been thrown into.

John stared out the window and watched the fires slowly die out and the once charming town reduced to giant, smoking cinder blocks.

Eddy was looking out the window as well, but his eyes were fixed on the hordes of undead which shuffled blindly through the debris littering Main Street.

"You holding up okay?" John asked when he saw the kid's eyes starting to tear up.

"Yeah, I'll be all right. I just haven't had time to take this all in yet. You know, process it. Just yesterday I was thinking about where I wanted to go to college, and now I'm wondering if I'll even live through the night. Ever since my dad drove us here, I haven't stopped. And now that I've finally stopped, I kind of wish I was busy again, so my mind wouldn't have to think."

"Just hang in there, son. I'm going to get us out of this mess."

"I hope you do, Sheriff, but I don't think you will. Nothing personal, but I'm all out of hope."

"Well, I'll do my best," John said. He heard June cough and saw her sit up suddenly. She brought a hand over her month and her chest rose up and down as quick, violent coughs rocked her diaphragm.

"You okay, June?" John asked.

She nodded her head but still the coughs came.

"Can I get you anything?"

"I could use some water," she choked.

"I'll be right back." He left the room and walked down the hallway.

The water cooler was situated in the hallway near the stairs leading to the first floor. As he walked toward it, he saw that the five gallon bottle was nearly full with clear, crisp water.

A stack of blue paper cups sat atop the bottle. John removed a cup and filled it.

The light cough of someone caused him to turn his head.

"Oh, I didn't mean to startle you," Samantha said.

"It's okay, Sam. What's up?"

He saw the tears rolling down Samantha's pretty face and immediately put the cup down and went to her. She buried her face into his chest and began to cry.

"Why? Why is this happening?" she sobbed.

"I don't know. I just don't have an answer. I'm thinking terrorists but why the hell would they attack a nowhere town like Cypress Pass? Hell, I'd be shocked if they even knew it existed."

"But…they're all dead out there! Dead, John! Dead people don't wake up," she said, this time her voice more composed. "Everyone is dead."

"Who is, Sam?"

"My friends. I saw one in the diner. She was the cutest little girl and I'd just seen her two weeks ago. But what I saw in the diner was a monster."

"You don't know about your friends. For all we know, there could be groups of people out there like us; hiding somewhere, just waiting to be rescued."

"You don't believe that," she replied bitterly.

He placed his hands around her face and his cool hands felt refreshing on her hot cheeks. His steely blue eyes locked onto hers.

"I have to believe in something, Sam. For the first time in my life, I'm truly scared and I don't have the answers to anything. But I do know this, we've made it this far. We're safe. And I believe other people out there are safe, too. And I'm going to make sure you stay safe."

A single tear rolled down her cheek but John caught it with his thumb before it fell to the floor.

"Trust me when I tell you that I'm going to do everything in my power to keep it that way." He slowly brought his face to hers.

Their lips met and John could feel her body rise up and her lips press firmly against his.

He could feel the electricity shoot through his body and he knew she was feeling it as well. Their lips broke and she hugged him tightly.

"Thank you," she whispered.

"You have nothing to worry about," he replied.

The sound of Mayor Dunlop's scream killed the mood instantly.

"Stay here!" John yelled and rushed to the conference room.

43

John charged into the room, confused by the chaotic scene. He saw Mike, Kelly, Eddy, and Roger huddled in one corner of the room with Dunlop across from them. He appeared to be fighting with Simone.

"Goddamn it, will you idiots get this crazy bitch off me!" Dunlop screamed.

The mayor was holding one of Simone's arms at the wrist and his other hand was firmly around her neck. A river of red blood flowed from a tattered wound on his right forearm. Simone issued a raspy moan. John ran over and pulled Simone off of Dunlop. She fell back and hit the wall so hard that John heard her head crack into the plaster.

"The old bat bit me! She fucking bit me! And all you bastards did was watch!"

Simone staggered to her feet, her raspy breathing filling the room. She let out a low moan and lunged forward. John spun around and firmly gripped her throat, slamming her hard against the wall. Loose chunks of bloody flesh dripped from her mouth and her mouth snapped forward at him. Her eyes were the color of sour milk, cloudy with a greenish-white hue. He pressed his gun against her forehead and pulled the trigger. Her blood splashed his cheek from blowback, her body immediately going limp. He released her and she crumpled to the floor with a sickening thud. Wiping the blood off his face with his shirt sleeve, he gazed back at the group.

"Is everyone okay?"

John glanced at Mike and he nodded his head. John looked down and noticed June was under the table again. Samantha was standing in the doorway, her hand over her mouth in shock, her eyes wide.

"No, everyone is not all right, John! She just bit me!" Dunlop screamed. He ran over to where Roger was standing and thrust his bloody arm into Roger's stunned face. Blood lightly rained down on the white tile floor from the gaping wound.

"You see! You see this, asshole! I told you! I told all of you what would happen if we let them in!" Dunlop pointed an accusing finger at Eddy, who looked as if he'd just released his bowels.

"You're worthless, son! You're a spineless sack of horse crap! They came in and now we're all going to die!"

Dunlop then set his focus on John. He rushed over and pushed him.

"This is all your fault! You're terminated, Sheriff! Get the hell out of my town! And take your retched friends with…" Before he could finish, a fist struck him in the jaw and dropped him to the floor. John looked over at Roger, who was rubbing his sore hand.

"I've been waiting to do that all day," he said.

John looked down at the rumpled mass that was the unconscious mayor of Cypress Pass.

"What should we do with him?" Kelly asked.

"I'm not sure, maybe just let him wake up and see if Roger knocked some sense into him," Mike added.

John went over and knelt down beside the lifeless body of Simone. What happened to her to make her go crazy like that? As he looked her up and down, he then saw it. A greenish fluid was slowly dripping from her leg wound and pooling on the floor. He lifted her cotton dress back and saw the white bandage he'd placed on her leg was now completely soaked through with a green, foul smelling pus. The smell of putrid almonds hit him and he connected the dots.

"Get away from him!" John barked, causing everyone to jump and move away from Dunlop.

"What's wrong?" Samantha asked.

"He's been bit. Today, I was attacked by two old people, both with bite marks all over their bodies. Later, I rescued a man and he was bit. About an hour later he was trying to kill me. Then Simone got scratched badly by one of those things and she changed. There's some connection with them breaking our skin. They're infecting us and when that infection takes hold, we become like them."

"Well, if that's the case, let's just kill him now," Roger said, the pleasure in his eyes apparent.

"We can't do that," Mike said.

"And why the hell not? He's been a complete prick since we got here. And now you're telling me he's gonna come back like one of them? So what? We'll have a cannibalistic, asshole prick soon?"

"He's still human. He hasn't changed yet," Mike said flatly.

"But for how much longer? You want him to be in the room with us, Mike? With Kelly?"

"No I don't want him in here, but that doesn't mean we have to kill him. We don't know if what John said is even true."

"But it's a risk we can't afford to take," John said, finally entering into the conversation.

"Then what do you want to do, John?" Mike asked.

"We could put him in one of the holding cells?"

"I really don't feel like lugging his big ass downstairs," Mike rebutted.

"Then what about one of the interrogation rooms up here? They lock from the outside so we won't have to worry about him getting out," John suggested.

"Hey, that's not a bad idea," Mike said. "Roger, give me a hand with him."

With Mike lifting his shoulders and Roger lifting his legs, the two hoisted Dunlop off the floor. Through their grunts and groans, they were able to carry the limp mayor down the hall and into one of the interrogation rooms. The room was simple, containing only a two-way mirror, a small square table, and two chairs. They put him down gently and quickly exited the room. Mike locked the door and gave it a quick tug to ensure it was indeed secure.

Back inside the conference room, John was planning to get rid of Simone's unsightly corpse. With the help of Eddy, the two carried her to one of the windows.

"Turn around, ladies, please. You might want to cover your ears, too," John told the three women as he and Eddy slid Simone out of the window. He hated doing it to her, knowing how disrespectful it was, but there was no choice given the circumstances.

The body dropped like a limp rag doll falling from the hands of a child. It hit the ground with such a sickening crack that Samantha winced slightly even though her hands were firmly placed over her ears. Simone's head popped open upon impact, spilling red liquid and bits of brain matter all over the street. A group of zombies slowly shambled over to the fresh corpse, but recognizing it as one of their own, promptly turned away and continued their icy stare at the second-story window.

John closed the window and looked at the group. No one knew what to say, as all were at a loss for words. Roger and Mike had made their way back into the room and both had witnessed the tail end of what happened. June was hugging Eddy, weeping quietly; more for the passing of Simone than the quarantine of her husband.

John looked at his watch and saw it was only one in the morning.

"Guys, we have about five hours till it's sunlight. We should really try to get some rest. Any volunteers for watch?"

"I'll do it," Roger offered, which surprised John.

Roger turned to Eddy, who readily handed him his shotgun.

"Get some sleep, bro," Roger told Eddy. "I got your back."

"I'll stay up, too," Mike said. "You need to get some sleep, John. You've been going non-stop since this all began."

"I'll try, but I doubt I'll be able to sleep much," John said. He was lightly snoring within a minute of closing his eyes.

44

Though John had fallen asleep quickly, his rest was anything but pleasant. His mind was playing awful tricks on him. Loud pops of gunfire followed by the sounds of screams haunted his dreams. He was back inside the bunker, tied to the chair that he was lucky to have escaped once. But instead of Scarface with the chunk of wood coming to smash his legs into shards of broken bone, there was a rotting corpse, hungrily licking its lipless mouth in anticipation of a feast that was soon to come.

The corpse moved closer to him, and when it grabbed his hand, John jerked awake. His hand, now suddenly free of the restraints that had trapped him, was in a tight ball as he was about to bring it toward the corpse's rotting face. But the face quickly changed, and before his fist connected, he saw it was Samantha.

"Jesus, John, it's me," she said and jumped back, startled. "You were having a nightmare."

"Samantha." He let out a sigh of relief. "You can't wake me like that."

"I'm sorry. It's just…you were starting to worry me."

"It was that bad, huh?"

"You were talking to yourself. And you were making this horrible gurgling sound. I thought you might have been choking or something."

"First time sleeping sober in a while," he said, trying to lighten the mood a little.

"Do you want me to lay with you? It might make you sleep better, and I know I'd feel a lot safer if I could. I mean, I understand if you…"

"It's okay. I'd like that."

He held his arms open and she scooted her body into his. He could feel her warmth as she pressed into him, and he could smell the sweet aroma of lavender from her hair.

She placed her head on his chest and she felt his heart beating in a rapid rhythm. It didn't take long for the rhythm to resume to a normal beat.

"Why did your wife leave you?" she asked, the question catching John by surprise.

"Excuse me?" he said, unsure he'd heard her correctly.

"I'm sorry. I don't mean to be so forward, but not much stays a secret in our small town. Old women get to talking and soon the truth becomes something entirely different."

"No, it's fine," he said. "I just haven't talked about it for a while. To anyone recently."

Samantha slowly rubbed his chest softly.

He let out a deep breath. "Well, it was back when I was in Iraq. It was my second tour…"

"You went back?" she interrupted.

"I wasn't given much of a choice, but to be honest, I volunteered to go again. I just had to. It's a feeling I can't describe to anyone. The only times I felt truly alive and needed was on the battlefield. I just needed to be there."

"So you think she couldn't handle it?"

"No, she could handle me being gone, but it was the person who came back that she couldn't be around. That and we had a daughter. I guess it was just too hard on her."

"I didn't know you had a daughter."

John reached his right hand into his back pocket and retrieved his wallet. He flipped his badge back and under it was a small picture.

"Oh, she's precious," Samantha whispered.

Indeed she was. In the picture was the most perfect blond-haired girl, with a big smile that could melt anyone's heart. She was sitting on a bright pink bicycle, equipped with training wheels and streamers on the handles. A pink helmet sat atop her head and two long pigtails flowed from under it. John was kneeling next to her and had a smile that only a father could make.

"What's her name?" Samantha asked as she continued to study the picture.

"Jenny."

She handed the picture back to him and he tucked it back inside his pocket. He was fighting the tears that were starting to well up in the corners of his eyes.

"When we get out of here, make sure you tell her hello for me," Samantha said.

"You can tell her in person when you meet her."

She nestled her head on his chest and closed her eyes. John hesitated for a moment as he stared into the darkness of the room. He wondered where Jenny was and hoped she was safe. He let out a deep breath and closed his eyes. They were both asleep in minutes, and this time, he didn't dream.

45

Mike stood guard at the entrance to the conference room. He was sitting on a rather uncomfortable wooden chair and was doing his best to fight off the urge to sleep.

His head would start to droop downward and he could feel the lulling call of sleep sing to him like a siren to a shipwrecked sailor. However, the thought of what would happen to him if he gave in to the feeling always made him snap out of it.

He looked across to where the other 'guard' was resting. Roger was snoozing in the opposite corner of the room, his shotgun cast aside without regard.

Fucking useless, Mike thought.

Suddenly, Mike's ears perked up to a distinct noise in the distance. What had been a dull, faint whir was now the unmistakable sound of metal blades sweeping the humid night.

Helicopters! he thought, growing as excited as a little boy on Christmas morning. *We're going to get out of here!* He ran over to where John and Samantha were peacefully sleeping. He didn't wake John up as gently as Samantha had.

"John! Wake up," Mike hissed into his ear.

John sat up with a start. Samantha rolled off him and hit the floor with a soft jolt.

"Damn it, Mike. What is it?"

"Listen."

At first John thought Mike had gone crazy but then he heard it, too. "That's a helicopter," he said and got to his feet. He felt dizzy for a moment as he gained his equilibrium, but a second later it passed and he was moving to the window with Mike right behind him.

He could see the faint glow of red lights in the distance as two helicopters slowly made their approach. John flung one of the windows open and began to wave his arms like a mad man. Mike opened the other window and joined him.

The commotion woke the others. Outside the building, on the street, the dead, who had all but forgotten the reason they were smashed against a brick building, once more began to renew their activity.

"What is it?" June asked.

"Helicopters," Mike said. "We have to make them see us."

"I think it's too dark," June added, thoroughly raining on their parade.

"The hell it's too dark," John said and ran out of the room to retrieve one of the flare guns sitting on a table.

John aimed the flare gun directly in front of the helicopters' paths and fired. A streak of demon-red illuminated the sky.

Below, the dead were whipped into a sadistic frenzy as they licked their cracked lips, foamy saliva spilling freely down their chins.

The helicopters, however didn't seem to notice, and they continued their slow flight into the night.

"Damn it!" John yelled. "No way they didn't see us!"

He loaded another flare into the gun and fired. The helicopters' trajectory stayed the same. John could see the aircraft drawing closer and soon they were past the police station and completely out of sight.

"Damn it!" John yelled, spiking the flare gun into the floor in anger. The gun broke apart, pieces flying off in different directions.

"Come back!" Eddy screamed in desperation into the night. "They have night vision on those things! And infrared! There's no way they didn't see us!"

"At least we know someone's out there," Roger said.

"How comforting," John sneered. "A rescue crew that won't rescue us."

"Maybe they were assessing the situation and will be coming back to get us later?" Kelly mused.

"I doubt it," Mike said. "They would have at least called to us or something, maybe signaled with their running lights that they'd seen us."

"What if they don't come back?" Samantha asked.

"They have to, right?" Kelly said, her voice thick with doubt.

"I have a bad feeling about this," John muttered and closed the windows to block out the moaning of the dead.

"What if we got on the roof and made a signal or something?" Mike suggested.

Kelly nodded her head, liking the idea. "That could work."

"Sure, it, you know, in case they do come back," Mike said.

John checked his watch. It was almost four in the morning.

"There's no telling how long it'll be until they return and even if they will. But if they do come back, we need to be ready for them," John said.

"Well, we could wait on the roof," June added.

"Yeah, we could all go to the roof. If they fly over again during the day, they'll have to see us," Kelly said enthusiastically.

"By noon it's usually creeping on one hundred degrees. With the heat kicking off that roof, it'll be close to a hundred and twenty. We can't stay out there all day," John said, lowering the hammer.

Dejected, Kelly walked away and put her hands to her temples. She began to rub them up and down, trying to fight off the headache that was welling in her head.

"Whatever, I don't care what we do!" Kelly yelled. "I just want to get the fuck out of here!"

"I think we should try to make a break for it," John said quietly. "I don't like how those helicopters passed us up without so much as investigating. No one would ever do that on a rescue mission. There's something very wrong going on and I don't want to stick around to find out."

"Wrong?" Mike asked rhetorically. "You mean besides the dead walking?"

No one replied to him.

"John's right. We have guns and plenty of bullets. We could easily get away from them," Samantha agreed, standing next to John for support.

"And how are we going to get past them?" Eddy asked.

"You dumb ass," Roger said to Eddy. "Your dad's Tahoe is parked out back. We can all fit in it."

"It's worth a shot," John said. "What do y'all think? Should we make a run for it or stay here?"

No one disagreed.

"Okay, fine, but we need to create a diversion of some sort," Mike said. "Maybe I can shoot at them and get 'em all riled up; Roger can help me. That way when we come driving out the back, they'll all be focused on where we were shooting."

"That's not a bad idea, Mike. Maybe send up a few flares at them, too. We have more flare guns in the armory. We should be able to slip out the back with no problem," John said.

"And you're sure they'll fall for this?" Samantha said.

"Sure, it's not like they're smart or anything," Roger snapped as he paced the room.

"Just relax, Roger. We need to think about every possible out-come before we go through with this," John said.

Mike was staring out the window again. This time he was look-ing past the howling zombies, the burning town, and beyond where the wooden sign rested in a splintered mess. He was focus-ing on the bayou.

"You think they can swim?" Mike asked as he turned and faced the group.

"I doubt it," Roger said. "They can't climb, they can't break down doors; I really doubt they know how to swim."

"Well then, let's assume they don't. The bayou is only about five blocks away."

"Then what? We swim for it? There's a lot of shit in that water just as dangerous as those things out there, Mike. Hell, just last week the Rainey boy shot a twelve foot gator. We'd need a boat."

"What about the launch? They have boats down there all the time," Eddy added.

"The Fontenot's have a houseboat down there. I saw it docked yesterday and I hate to say it, but I saw Maria Fontenot in the diner yesterday. I don't think she made it. It could still be there," Samantha said.

"That isn't going to work," John said glumly. "A houseboat takes way too long to get started and moving. They would be on us before we could get off the dock."

Roger's pacing came to an abrupt halt and he walked up to John with an angered look on his face. "Then what the hell do you think we should do, huh? You've shot down every single idea we've thrown out so far!"

"Just because it's an idea, it doesn't mean it's a good one!" John fired back.

The two looked like their conversation might quickly come to blows, and for Roger, the outcome would not have been a good one. Then John had another idea.

It was such a simple solution to their dilemma that he almost thought of hitting himself for not thinking of it in the first place.

"We could use the SAR boat," John said.

"What the hell is that?" Eddy asked.

"Our search and rescue boat," John said. "It's definitely big enough for all of us."

"And where is this boat located?" Eddy asked.

"It's in a boathouse down by the docks," John said.

"Hot damn!" Roger smacked his hands together. "Let's get the fuck out of here!"

"I thought we were going to wait till the morning?" Kelly asked, sounding more worried by the second.

"No way! Fuck that! I want to get out of here now!" Roger yelled.

"I think we should wait," Samantha added, and Kelly gave her a smile of gratitude.

Roger started pacing around the room furiously.

"This is something new we're about to try," John said. "We have to make sure everything goes according to plan." He was growing angrier with Roger with each passing second.

"Screw your plan and screw you! We can make a plan on the move!" Roger screamed in John's face.

John had had enough. His hands shot forward like an eagle snatching a small rabbit from a field, and gripped Roger's shirt. John could feel his muscles tense and flex as he brought Roger closer to him.

His eyes were burning a hole into Roger, and the kid was too scared to look away.

"I know you don't give a shit about anyone here but yourself, but I do. This is my town and these are my friends, and I'm going to do everything I can to protect them. You have two choices: you can either shut the fuck up and do exactly what I say…" He shoved Roger toward one of the windows, the action clear. "Or you can get the fuck out. I'd be happy to help you."

Roger turned away stunned and frightened.

Never in his life had anyone stood up to him like that. And if they tried, he would have readily fought them. But he knew John was a fight he had no chance of winning.

"This is all so fucked!" Roger screamed and slammed his fist into one of the walls, plaster raining down, a small dent left behind.

Suddenly, a thud answered Roger back. They group all turned and looked around, puzzled by where the noise had come from. Then they heard it again, this time from the hallway.

"I think the mayor wants to come out," Samantha whispered, and June gasped at the thought.

John walked quietly to the door. With each step he took, a pound on the door to the interrogation room seemed to answer him. He put his ear close to the door.

"Mayor Dunlop…It's John…You all right in there?"

What answered him wasn't Dunlop, well, not anymore. He could hear the wheeze of air flowing through dead lungs, followed by a low growl.

Suddenly, the pounding on the door became louder and more intense. John stepped away, swallowed deeply, and walked back to the conference room.

"Well, I guess our little theory was correct," he said and everyone knew what he was referring to.

"What do you want to do with him?" Mike asked.

"I don't know. Guess we could just leave him in there. He can't hurt anyone," John said.

"But what if someone comes in here and opens that door?" Kelly said. "They could get attacked. That's not right."

"He was a terrible person," June said. "But he doesn't deserve to be like that forever."

John turned to Eddy and he nodded in agreement. What struck John as odd and maybe a little sad was how well Eddy and June were taking the news that Dunlop was dead and had returned as one of *them*.

"All right," John said, looking at Mike, "Let's make this quick." He turned to the others. "Stay here, we'll be right back."

John and Mike slowly walked to the door like two executioners ready to carry out the sentence.

Mike placed the key inside the lock and slowly turned it. He could hear Dunlop on the other side pressing his hands to the door.

John was facing the door with his back to the wall, his shotgun ready in anticipation of what would come next.

Mike turned the handle and felt the door start to open. With a swift motion, he opened it, lifted his boot in the air, and kicked Dunlop in the chest.

Dunlop, unaware of what was going on, was thrown into the wall like a sack of clothes.

John quickly entered the small room and took aim.

Dunlop's milky eyes focused on John for a brief moment before his entire head evaporated into a red mush, the sound of the gunshot echoing in the small confines, making everyone's ears ring.

As the report of the shotgun exploded off the walls, the group in the conference room all jumped in surprise.

John looked down at the former mayor. The bite on Dunlop's arm had begun its morbid spread.

Red foam pulsated from the dark purple wound, green veins twisting their way up the arm, lost underneath his shirt.

"Come on, let's get back to the others," John said and left the room. Mike followed, closing the door and locking it out of habit.

The two men reentered the conference room.

"It's over, he's dead for good," John said softly as all eyes focused on him.

The reign of Mayor Dunlop had come to a violent end.

46

"So we all understand what we're doing, right?" John asked, the other members of the group nodding their heads in agreement.

Mike and Roger took the positions near the open windows, both holding a loaded pistol and a flare gun.

"Okay, Mike, you and Roger just unload on them. Get them all worked up and concentrating on where y'all are standing. Make as much noise as possible."

"Got it, boss," Mike said.

Roger remained silent, his jaw tight.

"The rest of you follow me, and stay close. We're gonna make our way down the stairs and to the back door. Once there, everyone will get inside the truck while I run to open the gate. When I get inside the truck, I'll honk the horn three times for you, Mike. When I do, you and Roger come running down. I expect y'all to be sitting next to me in less than a minute. Then we drive off and get to the boat shed where our boat is waiting. Once in the boat, we'll drive till we get to safety. Everyone understand what I've said?"

"Yes," "Got it," "Sounds good," "Let's do this," everyone said at the same time.

"Okay, on my count... One...two...go!" John yelled as Mike and Roger opened fire into the undead crowd below.

The bullets streamed through the night. Most of them landed harmlessly on the ground and ricocheted off the concrete and into the surrounding buildings. Others found their marks and inflicted damage on the animated corpses.

The dead were bewildered and intrigued by the unexpected display coming from above them. Their ears could hear noises and their cloudy eyes could detect flashes of light which drew them closer in a hypnotic state. The hunger inside them was raging, and they knew that whatever was causing the commotion, would make a pretty fine meal.

"Mike, check this out!" Roger yelled as he shot a flare into a cluster of zombies.

The red flare streaked toward them and struck a zombie standing near a large, green dumpster. Immediately the creature went up in flames. Roger let out a loud laugh. Mike wasn't sure if the creature could feel pain, but he saw it thrash around and latch onto a nearby body, igniting it as well. The scary part to Mike was that Roger seemed to be enjoying it. Mike took no pride in shooting at the people that just yesterday he would have said hello to.

John was quickly moving down the stairs. Behind him trailed Samantha, Kelly, June, and Eddy. He made a sharp right when he reached the bottom, the group snaking their way down the hall. John was relieved no one was being held in custody at the moment as he would have had to deal with it.

He approached the small metal door and placed his hands on the bar running across it. Pressing forward on the bar, the door opened. The group stepped out onto a concrete parking lot which held only one vehicle: the pearl black Tahoe of the former mayor of Cypress Pass.

Large spotlights illuminated the small parking area and a ten foot tall, chain-link fence formed a safe enclosure. John looked back and forth but didn't see any zombies around the perimeter. He ran over to one of the electrical panels positioned near the metal door and snapped off the overhead lights, while June fumbled in her pocket for the keys, producing them a moment later. In the distance, the gunfire still echoed as Mike and Roger continued the distraction.

Suddenly, the gunshots ceased and the taunting yells of Roger and Mike echoed through the air.

"They must be out of ammo," John said. "Come on, guys, get in the truck. I'll unlock the gate."

They piled into the Tahoe and John went sprinting for the gate. He reached it and fumbled with the padlock. The gate gave a low metallic groan as he slid it open. Turning, he ran back and jumped into the Tahoe. June had already started the engine and it was idling softly.

"Damn, Eddy, your father was driving around in style," John said upon seeing the leather interior, navigational system, DVD player, and all the other bells and whistles.

John put his hand on the horn and pressed it three times, hard.

47

"That's the signal," Mike said as he turned and ran out of the room with Roger at his heals.

They dashed out of the back door and Mike got into the front passenger seat next to John, while Roger sat in the first row in the back. The Tahoe fit them all comfortably with John and Mike in the front, Eddy and Roger in the two back seats, and the three women on the back bench.

"Here we go!" John yelled and stepped on the gas pedal, the Tahoe's massive engine roaring to life, the vehicle shooting out of the parking lot.

John made a quick right turn and drove down a small path of concrete which led to Main Street. He was already dreading the ride, and when he made the turn, his fears were confirmed. In front of him, the streets of Cypress Pass were littered with debris and the two classes of dead: the truly dead and unmoving, and the walking.

Everything looked so gray. From the ashen, burned-out buildings to the gray-black sky overhead. The residents of Cypress Pass were in the streets to greet the passengers of the Tahoe, only they were all now the living dead.

There had to be hundreds. The scene reminded John of a news clip of Bourbon Street in New Orleans during Mardi Gras. The throngs of walking corpses literally choked the road.

John cut sharply to the left and narrowly missed a group of zombies that were standing in the road. The next group wasn't as lucky. They formed a straight line which ran across the street. Their positioning reminded John of a morbid version of the school game 'Red Rover.' *Red Rover, Red Rover, send John right over,* he thought as the Tahoe plowed through the dead, crushing a small zombie girl in the process. The small body crunched and popped underneath the truck's large tires.

The part that made John the most queasy was that he'd chosen her on purpose, as he figured she would have been the easiest to get past. He felt the tires start to slip and was jarred suddenly by the side of one of the buildings.

"Fuck man, watch it!" Roger screamed out and Mike shot him a nasty look.

Then suddenly, John slammed on the brakes. He could feel his heart, which was already pumping fast enough to explode, quicken its pace again. There before the vehicle, was an army of the undead.

"What are you doing?" Mike asked. "Go!"

John pointed his finger forward and Mike followed it. He'd been concentrating on Roger and hadn't seen the crowd.

In front of the Tahoe was a wall of quivering flesh, dead eyes, and gaping mouths. John had to think quickly; he could only let the fear consume him for a few seconds. Five seconds passed, but they felt like five minutes to him, before he noticed a small gap where the sidewalk met the street.

"Okay, guys," he whispered, trying his best to remain calm. "I'm going to hit that small opening right there." He pointed. "Everyone hold on, it's gonna get bumpy."

Roger tapped Eddy on his knee and Eddy jumped slightly. Roger nodded his head to the side and gestured toward an empty alley. Eddy nodded in acknowledgment.

Roger mouthed, "On three," and began the count down with his fingers. On three, he flung open the door, jumped out of the vehicle, and ran into the dark night. Eddy quickly followed, turning to give June a look that said, *I'm sorry, Mom.*

"Roger! What the hell! What are you doing?" John screamed as the humid, rank air filled the cabin of the Tahoe.

But Roger didn't care to explain himself. He heard John call out but wasn't going to give the sheriff a response. He was focused on surviving, and there was no way he was going to make it trapped inside the Tahoe.

Eddy was running right behind him as they made their way to the open alley. A few zombies spotted them and attempted to give chase, but the speed of the two boys quickly separated them from the slow, walking corpses.

"Eddy! Don't leave me!" June cried, but Eddy didn't hear her.

When the two boys reached the opening to the alley, Eddy bent over and sucked in air. His lungs felt like they were on fire and his legs felt wobbly, like they were made of gelatin. He hadn't run like that in a long time, and it was nothing like the video games he spent hours playing.

"Well, what's your plan?" he asked Roger between gasps of air.

"We go around the zombies, man. We stick to this back alley and we'll be at the launch in five or six blocks. All those dead fucks are gonna be focused on the Tahoe; we'll get in unseen."

Eddy had to admit that sounded like a good plan, but he was bothered that Roger had failed to mention this to the group. This may have been one idea that wouldn't have been shot down. Eddy gazed back at the Tahoe and saw Samantha's hand reach out for the handle, then slam the door shut just as a zombie flung itself at the closing door.

"Should we at least try to signal them? Let them know what we're doing?" Eddy asked.

"Man, we need to take care of ourselves. The people in the Titanic who waited around for a lifeboat found themselves dead when they didn't fight to get a space. I don't know about you, but I want my seat on the lifeboat," Roger said.

Roger had been quoting *Titanic* a lot lately. He'd finally watched the movie a few days ago and Eddy thought his reason for leaving the car was pretty stupid; there was enough room for everyone. Either way, it was too late to go back now. The dead had closed the gap between the boys and the Tahoe.

48

"No, no, no!" John screamed as he slammed his fist onto the steering wheel.

The horn blared for a quick second each time his fist hit the wheel. "Those goddamn idiots!" he shouted.

"John, we have to get going," Mike said.

John knew Mike was right. If he delayed now, the Tahoe would be surrounded in seconds. With nothing else to do for the two boys, he stepped on the gas pedal and made his way for the small opening to freedom. He felt the jolt and saw sparks fly as the Tahoe clipped the side of a brick building. To his right he saw red splashes and bits of flesh pepper the Tahoe's passenger window as the soft flesh of the dead readily gave way to the surging metal of the Tahoe.

But there was a problem. As the walking dead fell, the tires spun and skidded under the ropey entrails and slippery juices of the crushed zombies. John could feel the engine struggle as he tried to get the SUV moving again.

"Use the four wheel drive!" June shouted and John shifted the lever in the console, placing it into gear.

He accelerated and felt the Tahoe move forward. Cutting the wheel hard, he drove down the sidewalk, taking out garbage cans, a mailbox, and any unlucky zombie that shambled too close.

Roger and Eddy were greeted by clear streets as they moved closer to the docks. They ran as quietly as they could, though Eddy's heavy breathing and wheezing was starting to become noticeably louder. As they drew closer to the docks, the smell of the murky water seemed to permeate the air. Roger could hear the sound of frogs and other night animals resounding louder in the quiet night. Then he saw the dark, wooden form of the boathouse.

"We're gonna make it!" Roger said as he pumped his fist into the night air.

John shook his head as he fought to control the Tahoe as it barreled down the street. He had to drive a little slower than he preferred to, as the streets were littered with debris that he had to swerve around.

"Those idiots don't have the key to get in the boathouse," John said.

"What?" Kelly asked.

"You don't think we leave the building for our SAR boat unlocked, do you?" John asked.

"I hope Eddy's all right," June said mournfully. "He's always been like this. He doesn't think before he does something, then deals with the consequences later."

Mike nodded. "Let's hope the consequences of his actions this time don't end up getting him and Roger killed."

"Yeah..." John trailed off. But deep down, he hoped they both got what they deserved.

49

Roger and Eddy stood dumbfounded before the locked wooden door of the boathouse.

"This can't be happening," Roger said and slammed his fist against the wood.

The door shook slightly but was far too thick to simply be kicked in. Like the police station door, it was solid and heavy, and unless he had the key, it wasn't budging.

"Fuck, it's locked!" Roger yelled as he stepped back.

"Locked?" Eddy said.

"Did I stutter? It's fucking locked! Not open! Closed! Fuck!"

"What do we do now? Can we get inside another way?" Eddy asked as he looked around, answering his own question.

The sides of the boathouse extended into the murky bayou. There was no way they could get to the other side without getting wet, and even then there were no windows to use to break into the building.

"You want to swim around?" Eddy asked.

"Dude, I'm not getting in that nasty water."

A low moan behind them pierced the silence of the night. They spun around together to face what they'd been running from. An odd group of three zombies lurched toward the petrified boys.

The first one Roger saw was a burly man, twice Roger's size. He stood almost an entire foot over Roger and gave off the look of a ravaged bear. He was accompanied by a small, frail, older woman who was missing half of her lower jaw. Her tongue flapped in the darkness. The third member of the group was a leggy blonde who had been quite beautiful before she died.

Her face was unmarked and she had a cute, upturned nose and high cheekbones. Her stomach, however, was a gaping hole where purple and gray organs wiggled from the gash to hit the ground with a splat each time she took a step.

"Shit!" Eddy cried and threw himself at the door.

The door hardly budged. Roger raised his shotgun and pointed it at Eddy.

"Hey, what the hell?" Eddy said, staring down the barrel of the gun.

"Damn it, will you move!" Roger yelled and Eddy dove out of the way, relieved he wasn't the target of Roger's aim.

The shotgun gave off a loud blast and a spark of fire as the shell obliterated the metal lock. What was left was a six foot wide smoking hole where the lock had been.

"Come on, move!" Roger snapped as he kicked the door open. After the two boys dashed inside, Roger slammed the door closed. Eddy was pacing frantically behind him, his eyes wide with panic.

"What do we do now?" Eddy screamed at Roger.

"Just help me keep this door locked!" Roger barked as he placed his shoulder against the door. He could feel the pressure being applied from the other side as the zombies tried to get in, and felt the door slowly push inward.

Eddy ran at the door, his arms outstretched, and pushed on it, closing the quickly opening gap. The moans from the dead on the other side iced his blood.

"We are so fucked," Eddy said as he kept pressure on the shaking door.

50

John arrived at the clearing that would lead to the docks and slammed on the brakes. The tires made no noise as the vehicle came to a sharp, but gentle stop. The boathouse was about a block away, and they would have to leave the SUV to get there.

"All right, guys, have your weapons out and ready. Stay behind me and we'll get there fine," John said as he put the Tahoe in park and turned off the engine. He left the keys in the ignition in case they needed to get back to it on the run. Besides if things went right, they wouldn't be returning anytime soon.

They all filed out and quickly formed a line behind John.

"Mike, watch our backs," John said and Mike quickly moved to the rear of the line.

John could hear the screams and moans of the walking dead behind them, but they had put enough distance between them to not worry for a while. He saw a few shadows stumbling slowly in the distance but he wasn't concerned with them. The group would be long gone before the first zombie arrived.

"Let's move," John whispered as the group stealthily walked to the docks.

Roger was pressing against the creaking door with all his weight. He could smell the sickly-sweet aroma of blood and death, and he tried his best to not lose his stomach contents in the bayou water. Eddy was on the floor, doing his best to serve as a human door stopper.

"Get in the boat!" Roger yelled to Eddy. "I think I can hold them off. Maybe there's a key or something in one of the compartments for it."

Eddy got to his feet and ran to the SAR boat, which was gently rocking back and forth in the dark water. It was a standard search and rescue boat for a small town police force. The flatboat measured nineteen and a half feet long and was constructed out of solid aluminum. It was light enough to sit on the water and move quickly but heavy enough to take a decent blow and not sink. In the center was the steering console which was covered by a fiberglass enclosure. The boat was striped with green and gold and had the bold SAR logo displayed on each side. Atop the center enclosure sat a row of red, white, and blue police lights. Twin Yamaha 150hp motors sat behind the boat, giving it ample power.

Eddy climbed into the boat and began frantically searching. He opened storage lockers and fumbled through dark crevices and openings. None of them produced a key.

"Anything?" Roger yelled.

"I can't find it!"

"Damn it, look harder!"

"Look harder? I've looked everywhere! Why would the cops leave the keys in the boat?"

Eddy looked at the water and let out a frightened scream. Bobbing in the water was a head, and with it a pair of eyes that were hungrily fixed on him. He blinked and suddenly the head was gone, a small path of bubbles tracing their way to the surface.

The large zombie slammed into the door. It wasn't so much an intentional move, but the zombie had stumbled and fallen forward onto the door. The sudden pressure caught Roger off guard and he almost stumbled forward, the door opening.

"Jesus Christ! Eddy, come help me!"

Eddy just sat in the boat. His eyes were fixed on the water as each little bubble silently popped on the surface.

"Eddy! What the fuck man! Help me!"

Eddy shook his head as if clearing it, then ran to Roger.

"Sorry, man, I thought I saw something. I couldn't find a key."

"I bet that damn sheriff's got it!" Roger groaned as he pushed on the door, his feet sliding on the wooden floor. He leaned into it and pushed back.

The zombies were howling and clawing at the door, as if they knew it was only a matter of time before they reached their meal.

John and the others made their way as silently as possible to the docks. Along the way, they encountered a few zombies, but decided to just avoid them instead of shooting, knowing gunshots would probably attract more of them. The few that had insisted on trying to get in a bite were greeted with the blunt end of a shotgun to the forehead. John saw the boathouse first, but wasn't prepared for what greeted him. Standing in front of the door were three zombies, all trying to get inside.

"That's where we need to be," John whispered as he pointed his gun at the zombies.

"How do we get around them?" Samantha asked.

"We don't, we go through them," John said. He crouched down low and slowly walked toward the three zombies. His pistol was in his hands and ready for action. A picnic table was just ahead of him and he settled behind it, then motioned for the others to follow him.

When they joined him, John said, "I'll draw them to me and take them out. Mike, be ready in case I miss." But he knew he wasn't going to miss.

John walked out from behind the table and began to whistle like he was calling a dog. The first zombie to take notice was the pretty blonde. She let out a moan and began making her way to him as quickly as her stiff legs would allow. A second later, the other two zombies turned and also followed.

The blonde was within five feet of John when June yelled, "Shoot it, John! What are you waiting for?"

John knew it was all part of his plan. Let them get so close that missing wasn't an option. As the blonde zombie took another step closer, John put her down with a hollow point to the head. The other two were right behind their fallen comrade, but John didn't wait for them to catch up. He went and greeted them each with a perfect shot between the eyes.

"Let's go!" John yelled and the others immediately followed.

Suddenly, John's attention was taken from the boathouse to the small patch of woods a hundred feet to the left. From out of the woods more than two dozen walking dead came forth, all with their cloudy eyes locked on their prey.

"Girls, get to the door and get inside!" John yelled as he handed Samantha the key to the boathouse. "Mike, help me buy us some time!"

Samantha ran to the boathouse door with June and Kelly right behind her. When they approached it, they saw the large hole where the lock should have been. Samantha pushed the door inward but it wouldn't budge.

"What the hell?" Samantha said as she tried to push the door again.

"Move aside," Kelly ordered and delivered a hard kick to the center of the door. It gave a little, but quickly snapped back.

"Who's in there? Let us in!" Samantha ordered as she and Kelly pushed on the door.

June stood to the side, too nervous to help.

John and Mike were doing their best to slow down the mass of zombies that seemingly appeared out of nowhere. They targeted the legs since it not only dropped a zombie but also caused the others to trip and fall over the downed ones. Once prone, it took a long time for them to find their footing again.

"Come on! Open the door!" Kelly pleaded.

From inside the boathouse, Roger sat with his back to the door. He had a foot against a wooden shelf and was perfectly wedged. The door wasn't going to open anytime soon if he had any say in it.

"Come on, man!" Eddy pleaded. "It's them! Let them in."

"I don't care!" Roger yelled. "They'll just let in more of those things! I'm not letting this happen again!"

"Dude, my mom is out there!" Eddy pleaded as he ran to the door and began to pull it open.

Outside, Mike aimed his shotgun at a zombie and fired, its face becoming nothing but a distant memory a second later. With that last blast he was out of shells. John had let a zombie get right in front of him before squeezing the trigger on his pistol.

Click.

John was surprised when the gun didn't fire. He was certain he'd kept track of how many bullets he'd used. He took a few steps back and removed the shotgun from his back. He readied it like a baseball bat. As the zombie got within range, he swung forward and smashed the butt of the weapon into the zombie's skull. A sick crunch filled the air and the zombie dropped heavily to the ground.

Inside the boathouse Eddy still pleaded, "Roger! Get out of the way!" Finally, Roger moved aside. As he rolled out of the way, he grabbed his shotgun that he'd placed on the floor. He aimed the barrel straight at the door as it burst open. Samantha was the first to enter and she stopped suddenly, her eyes staring into the shotgun's muzzle. She closed her eyes tightly and felt June and Kelly gasp behind her. She really wasn't sure if Roger was going to shoot, but she said a silent prayer as she waited for the end.

Suddenly, she was grabbed and pushed to the side. John had come to her rescue, and with a swift motion, he knocked the shotgun to the side with his left hand and delivered a punishing blow to Roger's face with his right hand. Roger fell back onto the cool, wooden floor. His mouth was already filled with warm blood.

"What the fuck, man?" Roger mumbled as blood poured down his chin.

John stormed forward and grabbed Roger's shotgun. He yanked Roger to his feet by his shirt collar.

"You little coward," he hissed. "I should blow your goddamn knees out and let you slow them down for us." He pushed Roger forward.

"Get in the damn boat, and so help me if you do anything stupid, it'll be the last thing you ever do."

Roger sat down in the boat. He rubbed his sore face but didn't make a sound.

John took the keys back from Samantha and handed them to Mike.

"Get it started," he told Mike, who jumped into the boat as Eddy helped the other women in.

As Eddy helped June, he could barely stand to look at her. Tears began to flow instantly down his cheeks. "Mom, I'm so sorry," he cried and hugged her.

"Just don't leave me again, son," she said and hugged him back. She then pushed back a little and slapped him so hard across the cheek that the sound resembled the crack of a gun. Spittle flew from Eddy's shocked mouth as he stared at his mother in disbelief.

"Don't you ever do that to me again," she choked as tears started to well up in her eyes.

Mike turned the key and the dual motors roared to life. He pressed another button and the motors slowly lowered into the water. Eddy undid the ropes in the back and Roger got to his feet and removed the front ropes. John pressed his back to the closed door, and felt the first zombie pushing its hands on it a few seconds later.

"Mike, start backing it out!" John shouted.

Mike did as he was told and the boat began to slowly move out into the dark bayou. John turned and let the door swing open as he ran for the boat. The first zombie spilled in and fell to the ground. As heavy feet began to trample the body into a mush of gore and viscera, John aimed low and fired the shotgun three times. Each shot severed leg bones and the zombie front line fell to the boathouse floor, causing the ones behind them to fall as well.

"Come on, John!" Mike yelled.

John ran down the dock and jumped into the boat just as it was pulling away. A group of zombies made their way to the end of the dock and John saw them fall into the water one by one. It was almost comical. He could see their arms raised and thrashing about, unsure what was happening. Soon, their lungs filled with water and the weight sent them to the bottom of the bayou. Mike placed the boat into forward and sped into the night as the passengers all breathed a sigh of relief.

"Mike, slow down!" Kelly pleaded as the boat sliced through the water.

Either Mike didn't hear her, or was ignoring her as he pushed the throttle even further up. The bayou was just a blur as they zipped down it. The only light was offered by the moon overhead, the water an inky black, the outlined shadows of trees dotting the landscape.

"Mike, slow the fuck down! And turn the spotlight on!" John ordered.

"It's too dark to be going this fast!" Kelly screamed.

"Damn it, I know what I'm doing!" Mike yelled.

"The bayou is full of stumps and other shit!" John snapped. "If we crash then it's all over, slow down!"

"I can see just fine!"

As if on cue, the boat struck a stump halfway submerged in the water. The boat went airborne for a split second and then landed awkwardly. Mike struggled to regain control as the boat swung back and forth.

Suddenly, it struck an embankment and capsized. The passengers were flung into the air as each yelled and screamed in fear.

John felt himself go airborne. It was only a few seconds before he hit the water, but it felt like an eternity. He was brutally jarred by the water as his body slammed into it like a car running into a brick wall. His head broke the surface spitting out the foul liquid and he began paddling weakly toward the shore. Luckily, he'd been thrown close enough to one of the banks and he reached it quickly. Crawling onto solid ground, he coughed up the water in his lungs, then collapsed onto the moist ground, his senses taking in the aroma of dirt and grass. He stayed there for another few seconds, coughing and sputtering until his lungs cleared.

Suddenly, he bolted up off the ground, not sure if he'd lost consciousness or not. Looking around, he saw Samantha sitting next to him, her figure nothing but a lighter shadow amongst darker ones. She was holding her knee as blood trickled down the side of it. Mike was pacing back and forth on the bank a few feet away.

"Kelly?" he called out, frantically searched for his wife.

Then Roger's voice was heard coming from the other side of the bayou.

"Hey! We're over here!"

Roger, Eddy, and Kelly were sitting on the edge of the bank. Mike's heart settled to a normal pace when he saw Kelly stand up and walk to the water's edge.

"Is my mom over there with you guys?" Eddy called.

"No, we haven't seen her," Mike replied.

"Shit!" Eddy shouted. "Mom? Mom, where are you? Can you hear me?"

"What do you want us to do?" Roger asked. "Should we swim across?"

"I wouldn't," John said as he stood up. "I saw those things falling in the water. They may be right under us and we'd never know it till it was too late."

Kelly looked across the bayou at the others and held her arms up. "Mike, what do I do?"

Mike looked at John who only gave him a shrug of his shoulders.

"I don't know. Just stay put for now," Mike said.

"What do we do, John?" Mike asked as he turned to face John.

"I really don't know," John said.

"I'm really sorry about the boat, John. I saw freedom and I just panicked," Mike said.

"Apologizing isn't going to change our situation. Just try to keep a cool head. This is what happens when you don't." He glanced at the others on the opposite bank and then back at Mike.

"They can either try to swim to us or they can keep walking and meet up with us when the land gets closer together."

Samantha had been walking up and down the shore looking for June. She returned empty handed and panicking. "I can't find June anywhere," she said.

"Hey, guys! Any luck finding June?" John called across the bayou.

"No!" Kelly replied. "We'll keep looking though."

Kelly began walking the shore just as Samantha had done. She cupped her hands and called out June's name but there was no answer.

"Maybe she walked away after she reached the shore?" Roger said. "You know, like she was dazed or something." He seriously doubted it, but he was trying to make Eddy feel better. He was a little sad that June was probably getting munched on at the very moment by either a gator or a zombie. She was good in the sack.

"We have to keep looking," Eddy said as he and Roger walked away from the water and into the thick vegetation lining the shore.

52

The air was humid and warm as Eddy and Roger trudged onward, looking for June. Their shoes squished in the soft ground and mosquitoes buzzed around their faces.

"Mom?" Eddy called as they walked forward.

"June?" Roger yelled into the night.

They entered a small area that was bare of vegetation. The area was unique in that all of the grass and small shrubs had been cleared in a perfect circle around a large mound of sticks and mud. A small canal was cut into the earth that led to the bayou. Water gently sloshed back and forth against the entrance. Eddy walked toward the large pile and began to climb over it. His hands and feet sank down as his weight snapped the small sticks woven inside the mud hut.

"June? Where are you?" Roger yelled.

The rustle of leaves made them both turn their heads in surprise. They froze like twin statues as their eyes fixed on the location of the noise. Another rustle seemed to come from the opposite side and again they turned their heads, afraid of what might be coming their way.

"Kelly, is that you?" Roger asked.

Nothing.

Deciding it was just an animal, Eddy continued to make his way up the mound of vegetation. He wanted to get as high off the ground as he could in the hopes of getting a better vantage point. Roger reached for his gun and realized he no longer had it with him.

"Eddy, what are you doing? Get down," Roger said quietly.

Eddy ignored him as he continued his climb. He didn't expect it when his hand went crashing through the pile. His hand stopped as it slammed into something that he could feel break against his fingers. He withdrew his arm and saw in the moonlight it was covered in a yellow substance that resembled snot. He peered inside and saw a gleam of white. Looking closer, he saw what must have been two dozen small, oval-shaped eggs. His heart was beating fast as he began to slowly back down the pile.

"We gotta get out of here, now," he whispered to Roger.

Roger didn't have time to respond. As Eddy finished his sentence, a large explosion of sticks snapping and leaves being trampled filled the air like a shotgun going off. Eddy saw the alligator emerge from the brush and make a beeline for Roger. It was probably the largest alligator Eddy had ever seen and the reptile's large jaws clamped around Roger's stomach. Roger never had a chance to scream.

With an animalistic fury passed down from millions of years of predatory evolution, the alligator tossed Roger around like a cat tossing around a baby bird. Its teeth dug into Roger's flesh, and each massive chomp of its powerful jaws shattered bone and punctured organs.

Roger only remained alive in the creature's jaws for a few unpleasant moments. The first hit was so violent that his breath left him immediately. The *whoosh* of the wind whipped by his head as he was tossed from side to side. His bones cracked and blood welled up in his throat, and he coughed blood with each breath. Just when Roger thought he might be able to scream, the alligator bit down one last time, severing his spine and popping his lungs. The blood shot forward out of Roger's mouth as his world went to black. Eddy had already taken off running.

53

Kelly heard a loud noise and the sound in the quiet night caused her to jump. For a brief moment, she thought maybe June had been found. Another chilling thought was that maybe a zombified June had found them. She didn't hear a scream so she assumed everything was right. She figured Eddy would have screamed like a woman had there been any danger.

John, Mike, and Samantha had heard the noise as well.

"Kelly? What's going on? You find her?" Mike called out.

She didn't answer as she slowly made her way to the source of the noise.

The mother alligator felt that the prey in its mouth was dead and tossed it aside. It wasn't happy that this thing had attacked its nest. It flung Roger to the side and saw the other attacker run off. It gave chase, not wanting the chance for the thing to return and try to eat the alligator babies nestled within the mound.

Kelly was making her way closer to the sudden noise when Eddy's screams caused her to freeze. She heard the crashing of brush and could see the thrashing of bushes as Eddy's dark figure drew closer.

"Jesus Christ! Run! Run!" Eddy screamed as he made his way out of the brush.

He could hear the powerful muscles of the alligator flatten the grass and small shrubs as it made its way closer to him. He erupted onto the bank and saw Kelly staring at him; wide-eyed and scared.

"Run, Kelly!" he yelled, pushing her out of the way with both hands.

She was surprised at the quick burst of strength and went sprawling to the ground, hitting her backside hard on an exposed cypress root. She rubbed her sore back as he wondered what was going on.

Then Eddy's pursuer revealed itself. Only a few feet behind him, the powerful alligator sprung from the bushes. Using its tail as a propeller, it quickly cut the distance between it and its prey. Eddy was moments away from jumping into the water to make a desperate swim for it when the alligator pounced. It shot through the air like a leather-bound missile and wrapped its crushing jaws around Eddy's flabby stomach. He didn't have a chance to scream as he felt himself pushed underwater. His first, and only gasp, filled his lungs with water and he was pulled to the bottom of the bayou.

The last thing Kelly saw was the alligator's large tail disappearing under the water. Large bloody bubbles quickly erupted on the surface and soon faded.

The alligator felt its prey go limp almost instantly as it reached the bottom and nestled down. It would wait a few more minutes just to make sure before it began enjoying its meal.

"Holy shit," was all John could muster as he watched the shocking display unfold.

Mike was staring dumbfounded at the water and Samantha had her hand firmly clasped over her open mouth. A faint, "Oh my God" could be heard escaping her lips.

"Kelly! The gator's busy with Eddy. Get over here while you still can! John and I will cover you!" Mike screamed as he ran knee deep into the dark water.

He could feel his boots sink into the soft mud and he retreated slightly. Kelly didn't answer him. She ran, dove into the water, and began frantically swimming to the other side, fear filling her as she expected to be dragged down and killed at any moment from below.

"Kelly, slow down!" John called. "Try not to draw attention to yourself!"

She heard his voice amongst the water splashing over her ears and brought her strokes to a slower pace. She also kept her kicking feet to a minimum. She briefly stopped at the capsized SAR boat and pulled herself around it. Below her, the alligator saw this new animal on the surface, but it was content with the current kill and didn't feel the urge to kill again. The alligator gripped onto Eddy's lifeless arm and performed its death roll. The arm snapped off without any effort.

As Kelly passed the boat, she came across a body floating face down. It was bobbing like a cork and she recognized the shirt; it was the same one June had been wearing. Momentarily forgetting about the fifteen foot reptile that was somewhere in the water, she turned the body over.

"June?" she said softly, knowing her friend was dead.

June's eyes were open, and they slowly shifted so she was looking straight at Kelly. They gleamed the milky white emptiness that Kelly had seen enough of already. Kelly screamed as June opened her mouth and a low moan billowed forth. Instinctually, Kelly dove under the water out of the reach of June's clawing hands. She delivered a powerful kick to June's torso and sent the woman under the water.

Now that she had lost the ability to breathe, June didn't notice that water was flowing into her stomach through her open esophagus. Soon, the water-logged zombie began its slow descent to the bottom of the bayou.

"Jesus, Kelly, don't stop! Swim, swim!" Mike screamed.

Kelly swam forward with all her strength. She swore she felt something latch onto her ankle and told herself it was just a stick and not a decrepit hand making one last effort to grab her and pull her beneath the surface.

The primal brain of the alligator had kicked in. Ignoring the feast it had in its mouth, the sight of thrashing limbs triggered a basic response: something was in trouble and the gator was going to kill it. The alligator made its slow rise to the top of the bayou and John saw the flat, black head break the surface in the moonlight.

"Shit! The gator's on the move!" John screamed and aimed his shotgun.

"Shoot it!" Samantha yelled.

"I can't! Kelly's in the way!"

"Kelly, baby! Swim! Swim with all your might!" Mike ordered, his heart on the verge of exploding with worry for his wife.

Kelly was only a few more feet from the bank, the shore growing closer with each passing stroke. Mike couldn't wait that long and went in to meet her. His strong hands grabbed onto her wrist and he pulled her the rest of the way. Mike helped her to stand as they got to solid ground. He scooped her up in his arms.

"Shoot it, John!" Mike yelled as he carried Kelly away from the water's edge.

John aimed and fired at the oncoming alligator. He wasn't sure if he'd hit his target, but he saw the reptile immediately dive under the water. He stayed poised with the shotgun, ready in case the alligator was planning a surprise attack.

It didn't return.

"Screw this," John said, letting out a sigh of relief.

He turned and walked to where the others had run to safety. Mike and Kelly were locked in an embrace so tight that he couldn't tell where one ended and the other began. Samantha was sitting on the ground, rubbing her sore knee. Kelly was sobbing into Mike's chest and John could hear him whispering that every-thing was going to be okay. He knew it was a lie but kept his pessimistic opinion to himself.

"Guys, I hate to cut this tender moment short, but we need to get moving," John said.

"What about Roger?" Samantha asked.

Kelly pulled her face away from Mike.

"Eddy and Roger went off together. The alligator must have gotten Roger first and then went after Eddy," Kelly said. "Other-wise he would have been here by now."

"Are we giving up on June? She's still out there," Mike said.

Kelly shook her head. "No, I saw her in the water. She was dead…but still moving. She's one of them now."

"Damn it," Mike growled, kicking a rock in frustration.

"Where do we go now?" Samantha asked.

"North," John said. "The bayou runs north to south. If we keep going straight, we'll hit the highway eventually. We'll stay away from the water and be extra cautious. I don't think this terrain will be favorable to those things. They can barely keep their balance on dry land let alone a muddy swamp."

"Oh yeah?" Mike asked. "Tell that to Eddy and Roger."

John ignored him. He was trying to be positive and Mike wasn't helping.

"So we just head north?" Kelly asked. "That's your plan?"

"That's the only thing I can think of. You're welcome to come up with your own idea, but I'm following my own," John said.

No one replied, so John began walking north. Samantha soon followed and Mike and Kelly brought up the rear, each holding onto the other, Mike knowing how close he'd come to losing her.

54

The four survivors walked through the bayou vegetation for what seemed like hours. The terrain wasn't nearly as bad as they'd imagined, and the further they got from the bayou itself, the firmer the ground became. The thick grasses and tall shrubs were difficult to maneuver around, and when they went straight through them, they were greeted by prickly thorns. The mosquitoes and gnats were also in full swarm and were excited that four walking blood bags had dared trek through their territory.

They had tried making small talk but the conversations always fell flat and quickly ran their courses. None of them wanted to discuss their theory on why corpses were trying to kill them, or talk about the loss of June, Roger and Eddy.

John was listening to the orchestral performance of the bayou fauna as they made their way deeper into the uncharted territory. In fact, the more they walked, the more the sounds of crickets, katydids, and bullfrogs were replaced by the sound of Zydeco. The faint sounds of the accordion and washboard grew louder as the group pressed on.

"You all hear that?" John asked.

"I've been hearing it for several minutes," Samantha said.

"Weird, coming from around here. Mike, have your gun ready. I don't know what we're about to come across, but let's be ready," John said and gripped the shotgun tighter.

They walked for a few more minutes until John noticed the flicker of lights in the dark night. "This way, and keep quiet," he said as they slowly walked to the source of the light and music.

Sitting nestled on Bayou Bouef was a small house, and it looked like someone was home.

"Should we go see who's there?" Samantha whispered.

"You're damn right we are," John said and began walking toward the small house. "Y'all just keep an eye out for any of those things."

The group walked cautiously toward the small home nestled in the dark swamp. John was in the lead, and when he reached the splintered wooden steps which led to a small patio, the music seemed to become louder.

The sounds of spoons rapidly beating on metal, accompanied by the high strings of a fiddle and the hollow sound of air rushing into a jug, danced around him in the humid air. He slowly walked up the stairs, his shotgun at the ready, and made his way to the tattered screen door.

Suddenly the music stopped and the sounds of crickets once again dominated the night. John's breath flowed heavily from his mouth as he aimed his shotgun at the door. The others had stopped dead in their tracks behind him the moment the music stopped. A thin whine filled the night and John realized the door was starting to swing open. He could hear someone behind him start to move, and assumed it was Mike, so he raised his hands for the person to stop. His eyes never left the now-open door. He could see the flicker of a lamp dance around the open doorway and he caught a glimpse of a couch, but nothing else. There was only silence.

"Hello? Is anybody in there?" he shouted, using his most authoritive voice.

No answer.

"This is Sheriff John Boudreaux! I know someone's in there! Come out now or I'll be forced to shoot!" he ordered, his finger caressing the trigger.

A black silhouette sprung forth from the darkness and entered the doorway. Had John been closer, he probably would have fired out of surprise. Lucky for him, he was far enough away to recognize the elderly lady who limped through the doorway.

The first thing John saw was that she was old, maybe in her nineties; definitely in her upper eighties. She had long, gray hair that hung around her skinny, shriveled face. She was wearing a tattered robe and had the appearance of an old witch. When the old woman opened her mouth to speak, she revealed a row of crooked, sharp teeth.

"What you want now? Go on, get outta here!" the woman ordered, waving her hands at them to leave.

"Ma'am, we're not here to cause trouble. I'm Sheriff John Boudreaux of Cypress Pass. Is there anyone else in the house with you?"

"Just me and my husband," she said with a thick Cajun accent.

"You shouldn't be here. It's not safe," John said.

"It ain't safe nowheres. Not with dem things runnin about and scarin' folk," the old woman replied.

"You've seen them?" Mike asked. He'd walked up the stairs to stand next to John.

"Lawd yes, I seen 'em. Ugly, devil people. Eyes sunk in like a coon and a mouth snappin' like a gator, yeah. Dey all hopped up on that dope I think."

"Did any of them hurt you?" John asked; his eyes were searching all over the old woman, looking for a wound but she was covered by the robe.

"Nah, bébé. Mon mari shoot 'em both dead. Deys kill my chien em baiseurs! We'd every right to shoot. Was self-defense and they was on our property!"

"How many were there, ma'am?" Mike asked.

"Deux," the woman replied as she held up two twisted fingers. "But mon mari shot 'em dead, yeah. We just push 'em in da bayou when they weren't goin' be gettin up no more. Figure they make a bon meal for a gator or somethin'. Doubt they'll be missed much.

Samantha walked up next to John and whispered, "This isn't right, I'm starting to get scared."

John still had his eyes locked on the old women, his shotgun still at the ready.

"Sheriff, you best stop pointin' that gun at me," the old woman said.

John slowly lowered the weapon. He glanced over at Mike and nodded for him to lower his pistol. The old woman didn't appear to be much of a threat.

"Now, how 'bout y'all come in and get cleaned up. But don't be makin' too much noise, mon mari is asleep in the bedroom. He got all excited dealin' with dem crackheads that he had to lie down for a spell."

Mike took Kelly's hand, leading her to the doorway and Samantha walked past John and entered the home.

John took one last glance into the darkness before he turned, and entered the house.

When John entered the home, the first thing he thought about was the old fishing camp he used to go to as a boy. A small room served as both a living room and a kitchen. A ratty and torn couch sat in front of a tiny television that looked like it hadn't been turned on in ages. Old black and white photos hung on the wall, and a small wooden table with four chairs occupied the center of the room, between the kitchen and living area. The kitchen had ancient, antique appliances and a small refrigerator that had handles secured by duct tape. Two flags, one representing the Louisiana State University Fighting Tigers and another showcasing the stars and bars of the Confederacy, hung in the windows as makeshift curtains.

"Come, child. The sink's over here," the old woman said as she led Kelly and Samantha to the kitchen area.

John saw that the condition of the counter tops looked similar to the ones in his own house. Beer cans were strewn about, along with used silverware and napkins. The thought made him miss his home a little.

"What's your name, ma'am?" John asked.

"Ma name's Mary LeBeau. Been livin' out here all my life."

"It's nice to meet you, Mary," Samantha said with a warm smile.

John walked over to the window and moved the purple and gold curtain out of the way. The sky was starting to turn an ashen gray. "It'll be morning soon," he said to Mike.

"You wanna hole up here for a while?" Mike asked.

"Probably be the best thing. We should try to get a little sleep, too. I'll stay up if y'all are too tired."

Mike nodded his head. He wasn't going to argue with John, he was exhausted. Mary sat down at the table and John walked over and joined her.

"Y'all care for some coffee? It's got chicory in it," she offered.

"That would be great," John said and Mary got up to put a pot on.

"John's going to stay up. So the rest of us need to get some sleep," Mike said to Kelly and Samantha.

"That sounds like a great idea," Kelly said, already eyeing the couch.

"Excuse me, Mary?" Samantha said.

"Yes, cher?"

"May I use your restroom?"

"Of course, cher. It's in the bedroom." Mary pointed to a closed door past the kitchen.

"It's on your left. Just don't wake Melvin. Lawd knows he needs his rest."

"Thank you. I'll be quiet," Samantha smiled.

Mary returned to making the coffee and began pouring water from a jug into the small coffee pot. She saw John's face as he eyed the water.

"Now don't you worry none, Sheriff. We buy our drinkin' water."

"Good to know," he said.

"So tells me, Sheriff, you a good cop or a bad cop?"

John was a little caught off guard by her question. "I try to be a good cop, ma'am."

"You try, but you don't always be a good cop, no?"

"Why do you say that?"

"Because no good cop could have a shotgun pointed at a li'l ol' lady like me."

John sat down at the table and put the shotgun down. He removed his pistol and began fidgeting with it. He always did this when he got nervous.

"Sometimes, the people you least suspect are the ones that kill you," John said, hearing the laughter of Iraqi children echoing in his brain.

"What kinda gun that is?" Mary asked.

"This? 9mm. Nothing special."

"What kind of bullets?"

"It's got hollow points."

"Why you usin' hollow points, Sheriff?"

"Because they go in clean and do a lot of damage."

"Are you like a hollow point, Sheriff?"

John's eyes locked onto hers. For a brief moment, he thought he saw his ex-wife staring back at him.

"Years ago, when I returned from the war, I wasn't too kind to my wife," he said. "You could say I came back quietly, but in the end caused a lot of damage. I've been paying for it every day since she left me."

"You got pain in dem eyes, Sheriff. Even a half blind woman like me can see that. But you got to live for da people who care for you," Mary said, glancing at the sleeping mass of Mike and Kelly. She glanced over her shoulder, where Samantha had disappeared on her way to the bathroom.

"I do the best I can every day, ma'am," John said with a smile as he loaded the pistol and set it down.

"I know. You's a good cop, Sheriff. I can tell."

56

Samantha entered the dark bedroom and quietly closed the door behind her. There was an open window above a small bed that let in just enough light for her to make out the outline of the room. The shape of a man was lying in the bed, his chest rising and falling with each deep breath.

She walked quickly to the bathroom and closed the door behind her, then flipped the light switch, the room becoming flooded with a bright, white light. She turned the knob for the cold water on the sink and began splashing cool water across her face. It felt exhilarating against her hot skin. Staring into the mirror, she watched the water slowly trickle down her face. She closed her eyes tightly and prayed she'd wake up, that everything that had happened thus far had all been a terrible dream and even now, she was home in her bed, wrapped in the bedcovers. She opened her eyes and stared back at herself. No such luck.

The sound of high-pitched coughing and wheezing echoed from the bedroom, causing her to jump. The sound was like a smoker's cough, lungs worn and full of mucus doing their best to clear some for a few more breaths of sweet air. The coughs continued and faded to a light gurgle. Samantha waited in the bathroom, silent and unmoving, until the noises stopped.

Water was dripping down her face and hands, so she opened the small cabinet under the sink to try and locate a towel. Only an extra roll of toilet paper and a stack of mouse traps greeted her. She looked at the shower, but no towel hung from the rod. As a last ditch effort, she thought there might be some towels behind the shower curtain, so she pulled the curtain back.

She'd been right. A crumpled pile of towels sat in the center of the tub. They were all mismatched in color and design, but one common theme they shared was the dark stain of blood going through them. The towels were so soaked that a small pool of red had seeped through the mass of cloth and was now making a faint trail to the drain. Samantha could feel her heart begin to race as she realized the predicament of her situation. The old woman had lied to them.

She drew the shower curtain closed. She had to warn John and fast, to get them out of the house before it was too late.

She wiped her hands on her pants and used the sleeves of her shirt to dry her face. It didn't help much, as her clothes were filthy, but she didn't care anymore.

After a few deep breaths, she was ready to open the bathroom door and enter the bedroom where she hoped the figure in the bed was still asleep.

Opening the door slowly, she did her best to make sure the door didn't let out the slightest noise as she walked into the dark bedroom.

The man was still lying in the bed, but this time his chest was no longer rising. She slowly walked past the bed and exited the bedroom with the same silence, her heart in her throat the entire time.

When she reached kitchen area, she saw John and Mary sitting at the table, drinking coffee and talking. She saw Mike's feet sticking out from where he slept on the couch and guessed Kelly was snuggled against him.

Samantha walked over to the table and lightly tapped John on the shoulder. "I need to talk to you, John…in private," she said softly.

John looked confused and Mary seemed a bit caught off guard by the sudden interruption. Samantha flashed Mary a reassuring smile. "It's nothing important, just something between us," she lied.

"Excuse us, Mary," John said and rose from his chair.

"It's no problem, young lovers. I was fixin' to do the dishes anyways," Mary said and brought the empty mugs to the sink.

Samantha took John by the arm and led him outside and onto the front porch.

He was mindful enough to make sure he had his pistol with him just in case there was trouble.

He could feel the wall of humidity wash over him as they stood on the badly-weathered, wooden porch.

The mosquitoes, excited by the emergence of a fresh meal, immediately swarmed around them.

John began to swat his face, already getting annoyed and wondering what was so damn important they had to go outside.

"Well, you have your privacy, so what's up?" John asked.

Samantha leaned in close to him. At first he thought she was going to kiss him and he was about to move his head to meet her lips, but instead she turned to the side and whispered in his ear. "I think Mary's husband was bitten by one of those things."

The words hit John like a sledgehammer to the stomach. "What? Why do you think that?"

"In the bathroom, the tub's full of blood-soaked towels. Her husband's in the bed and he was breathing funny, all raspy and like he was on his last legs. Then, when I left, he wasn't making a sound. He just stopped, like he'd died."

"Jesus Christ," John muttered, imagining the consequences if what she said were true. "Okay, let's go back inside. You wake up Mike and Kelly and I'll handle Mary."

The two reentered the house and Samantha immediately went to Mike and Kelly. She woke them gently and pressed a finger to her lips to make sure they were silent.

Kelly slid off Mike, who grabbed his gun to make sure it was still attached to his hip.

John walked over to the small table and slid his shotgun over to where he was standing. He stood with his palms pressed down.

"So, Mary, is your husband gonna be all right?" he asked.

"Yeah, he sleepin' like an ol' dog. He be all right in a few hours," she said, not looking up from the mug she was washing in hot, soapy water.

"Mary, listen to me. Did he get bit by one of those things?"

Mary stopped cleaning the mug, her hands starting to tremble slightly. "It...It was just a scratch. A small one on his arm. I cleaned him up real good. It happened so fast," she stuttered.

"Just a scratch?" Samantha said from across the room. "There's blood all over your bathtub? How did that come from just a scratch?"

Mary didn't have an answer.

"Listen to me, Mary, please. If he's been bit, he's gonna turn into one of them," John said softly, trying not to upset the visibly shaken old woman anymore than she already was.

"Turn into what? Some punk hopped up on drugs? Tell me how that's supposed to happen, Sheriff?" she asked.

John took a deep breath, dreading the words he was about to say. "Mary, I'm afraid I'm gonna have to shoot your husband."

57

"What? You can't do that? You've no right!" Mary yelled in shock as she began to cry.

"Listen to me, Mary, there's no other way. When he changes, and he will change, he'll attack you. He'll kill you! Or worse, you'll be one of those monsters."

"My husband is not a monster," Mary hissed with venom in her voice.

"Mary, please listen to the sheriff," Mike said, his hand still on his pistol.

"He's fine! It's just a scratch!" she screamed.

Kelly gripped Mike's arm, hard. The sudden confrontation was starting to frighten her.

"I want you people to leave my home! I was a fool to let you in! Get out, now!"

Mary flung open a drawer and began removing the contents and hurling them in John's direction.

He did his best to dodge the flying forks, spoons, and butter knives that sailed through the air.

"John, maybe we should get out of here!" Samantha yelled.

"Damn it, Mary, calm down!" John ordered as the flying silverware was replaced with spatulas, tongs, and a wooden spoon. *She starts throwing cast iron, and I swear to God I'm shooting her*, he thought.

When she ran out of things to throw, Mary went to the refrigerator and flung open the freezer door.

John thought she was going to start hurling food at him, and he was surprised when she turned around with a revolver in her hand. Without hesitation, he raised the shotgun and aimed it at her.

"Put the gun down, Mary. Don't do anything stupid!" John yelled.

"The stupidest thing I did was lettin' you people in here. Now get outta my house!"

"Mary please, we only want to help," Samantha said.

Mary cocked the revolver. "I said get out. Now!"

Suddenly, a loud boom thudded against the door separating the bedroom from the rest of the house. They all looked right at it, though John kept the barrel and his eyes on Mary, too.

"Melvin? You awake in there?" Mary called. "You see, we woke him up with all the noise we're makin'."

The rhythmic pounding on the bedroom door continued.

"I'm coming," Mary said. She lowered her gun and walked to the door.

"Mary, wait! You don't know what you're doing?" John yelled.

"I'm gonna let you meet my husband. He'll be none too pleased that you woke him up," Mary said while turning the door handle.

As the door opened, standing there was Melvin, but it wasn't the Melvin that Mary had been wed to for sixty-five years.

He was wearing light blue cotton pajamas, the kind commonly worn by elderly people; the sleeve covering his right arm was soaked through with black blood.

His eyes were clouded over and his once brown pupils were barely visible, the mouth curved into a permanent snarl.

"Melvin, you feelin' better, luv?" Mary asked with a smile. But her smile went away when Melvin lunged at her, his mouth open wide to take a bite from her exposed neck.

It happened so quickly John had no time to react. Melvin's mouth covered Mary's thin throat and his jagged, yellow teeth tore into her stringy flesh.

Mary was too frail to fight him off as he ripped at her throat over and over again, hot blood splattering the walls and dripping onto the floor.

"Oh my God, John! Do something!" Samantha screamed as Kelly dug her head into Mike's chest, not wanting to witness the awful scene.

John set his jaw and walked forward while cocking his shotgun. He aimed it at Melvin's head and pulled the trigger.

Melvin's head exploded like a putrid grape, the wall behind him becoming painted with blood and brain matter.

With Mary still in his grip, the two bodies slumped to the floor.

John looked down at Mary who was still twitching slightly. Her eyes were locked onto the ceiling and he wasn't sure she was even aware of what was going on.

He took aim and shot her. The roar of the shotgun pulsated throughout the house. As the report faded, he turned back to the group. "Let's go, now."

58

John, Mike, Kelly and Samantha stumbled through the dense vegetation once more, slowly and without purpose.

The recent scene at the old woman's house had left them deflated, and for the women, a bit heartbroken.

The fact that the zombies were everywhere had fully set in. It didn't matter if you were in a small city or a house in the middle of a swamp, they were always going to find you.

John didn't know it, but his three companions had all come to terms that the end was inevitable, but not him. He would never have that attitude.

He'd stared potential death in the face once in that cold, underground bunker, and when it stared back at him, he realized he wasn't afraid, that he wasn't going to give in to it.

Though they had only been walking for thirty minutes, it seemed like hours. Their arms and legs ached from the uneven ground, and the bugs swarmed around their heads like tiny, blood-starved kamikazes.

"We've got to be getting somewhere," Kelly said wearily as she slapped the side of her cheek, missing a mosquito.

"You can see the water's running south. If we keep going this way, we'll reach the highway," John said, though for some reason his confidence was starting to wan.

"I just wish we had flashlights. I keep falling in holes and running into shit," Samantha said.

John tried to flip the tactical light on the shotgun to 'on' but like before it wouldn't work. He looked up at the sky and appreciated the little light the moon provided. It was a clear night and the stars were on full display.

He stared up at them momentarily and wished he'd taken the time to look at them before. They were beautiful and plentiful, peppering the sky like golden confetti. He saw one of them begin to move and realized it was an airplane.

He imagined the people onboard staring out of the windows into black nothingness, not having a clue what was going on below them.

They continued their trudge.

An hour later, Mike said, "The ground's starting to thin out. It's only grass now."

Everyone had realized the woods had finally come to an end. A few more steps through the wilted grass and they were staring at the black asphalt of a highway.

"We made it!" Kelly cried triumphantly.

John even managed a small smile as he stepped onto the hard, flat surface. "No more walking in holes and muck," he said, and the others agreed.

The group stood in the center of the road for a moment before Samantha broke the silence. "Well, where to now?"

"We want to go east," John said. "Going west will only take us back to town, and I'm in no hurry to return."

They walked down the highway with John and Mike on one side and the women between them.

John had his shotgun at the ready and Mike had his finger on the trigger of his pistol. Samantha was clutching John's pistol and Kelly was holding onto Samantha.

On both sides, the treeline impeded their vision, the foliage thick and dense. The silent walk down the highway was more chilling than anticipated, for at any moment they felt something would be coming from them from the dark trees.

Fortunately nothing did, and their journey remained uneventful. They hadn't seen any cars, none fleeing from Cypress Pass in terror and none blindly driving toward it. This definitely struck John as odd since there were usually big rigs that passed through with their deliveries.

As they turned with the bend in the road, something caught their eyes. Peeking from behind the south treeline were four, large lights. They were so big and bright that they looked like little suns hovering in the night sky.

"What's that?" Mike asked.

"No idea," John said. "Never seen it before."

"Should we go that way?" Kelly asked.

"Shit, may as well," John replied. "It might be the Army or the National Guard."

John broke away first and walked off the highway and into the woods. The other three followed reluctantly, none of them excited about walking through the foliage and thorny shrubs again.

Luckily, it was a quick walk, and no sooner had they entered the woods then it broke into a field clear of trees. John got a better look at the lights and thought they looked like the ones that would light up a football field—big stadium lights.

As they got closer, a large American flag hanging limply in the windless sky came into view.

"Definitely military," John said softly.

Mike gave him a puzzled look. "Military? What would the military be doing with a base out here?"

As John started to answer, he was abruptly cut off.

"We made it!" Samantha cried as she leapt on John and hugged him.

Mike and Kelly embraced and Kelly silently cried into Mike's large chest. John gazed up at the bright lights and for a moment felt a reassuring calm rush over his tired body. The weary pack of survivors had made it. Nothing could spoil the moment.

That is until the savage cry of the undead coming from behind them split the night.

59

All four of them spun around at the same time to see a large group of shambling corpses pour out of the woods.

John couldn't count them all due to the shadows, but he estimated thirty on the low end and over fifty on the high.

The wall of living dead lurched forward across the field, their moans and wails piercing the once tranquil night.

John could hear the stomp and shuffle of feet dragging across the short grass and the sound reminded him of a herd of slow elephants.

He thought about making a stand and fighting. The zombies were slow, and with the field being large and open, he and his friends could easily dispatch all of the walking dead.

The girls would have to stand back; the end of his shotgun would do most of the work.

But before John could voice his plan, Mike yelled, "Run!" and grabbed Kelly's hand and ran toward the bright lights.

Samantha grabbed John and he had no choice but to follow. The lights were several hundred yards away and they sprinted across the field.

Halfway across, John's foot came into contact with something soft and yielding, and he went sprawling to the ground.

"Jesus, John! Are you all right?" Mike called as he stopped running and ran to help his friend.

"Yeah, I'm fine," John said and stood up, wiping his hands on his jeans. "I tripped over a sand bag or something."

"Glad you aren't hurt. Don't know if I could carry you," Mike said as he looked back toward the zombies.

They had put some distance between them and their pursuers. John walked over to the lump that had almost broken his leg. As he drew nearer, he realized it wasn't a bag at all.

He saw a set of two small arms and legs, a small torso, and face that looked like it belonged to a girl no older than his daughter. She lay on her back, her head bent at a horrible angle.

There was a bullet hole between her eyes.

As he looked around, he saw more black heaps strewn about the field. He walked to another next to where the first girl lay. It was a man, dressed in a plaid shirt and khakis.

He also had a bullet hole in his head.

Everyone realized they were surrounded by dozens of corpses.

John began to put the pieces together one by one: the lights, the bare field, the corpses.

This wasn't just an empty patch of ground, this was a killing field. Those bright lights were hiding snipers!

60

"Enough sight seeing, we need to keep moving!" Mike yelled as he and Kelly ran to the lights.

"No, wait, Mike! Stop!" John screamed, frantically running after them; Samantha trailed behind him.

But Mike didn't hear John's frantic calls. Both he and Kelly saw a flash of light come from just underneath the light furthest to the left. Mike didn't have time to think about the flash.

The second he saw it, his world went black instantly as the sniper bullet impacted his forehead, sending blood and bones fragments into the air.

He ran forward for a few more steps, his body not aware that its control center had been cut down, before finally pitching forward and sliding across the dew covered grass.

"Mike! Mike!" Kelly screamed, dropping down beside him, not understanding what was wrong with him. "No, no, no, no!" she cried while hugging his lifeless body.

The moment Mike went down, John pivoted back and tackled Samantha to the ground.

"Stay down," he hissed in her ear.

He looked over at Kelly who was rocking back and forth, sobbing and wailing into the night sky.

"Kelly, get down!" John screamed but she wasn't listening, too lost in her grief.

The sounds of the walking dead were slowly getting louder as John remained on top of Samantha, keeping her down. In a few moments, he would have to make a decision on want to do: either stand up and get shot by a sniper, or stay down and become a meal for the approaching dead.

He figured a bullet to the brain was a much easier way to go than a dozen festering jaws ripping away at his skin.

Then a plan came to him.

"I have an idea. On the count of three we're going to get up and run toward the zombies," he told Samantha.

"What? Are you nuts? That's crazy."

"No, listen. The snipers won't be able to focus on us. And we're much quicker than the zombies; we can run through them and back into the woods."

"What about Kelly?"

"I'll try to get her attention, but I think she's gone. Any will to live probably just died with Mike."

Samantha looked up and saw Kelly bent over Mike, not even moving, only her shoulders twitching as she sobbed.

"Jesus, you're probably right."

"I wish I wasn't. Okay, on the count of three we get up and run at the zombies. Run in a weaving pattern, not a straight line. It'll make you a harder target for the snipers, for all of them."

Samantha nodded.

"Okay, here we go. One…two…"

As John said 'three,' the screech of a rocket flying overhead drowned him out.

Without thinking, he threw himself over Samantha to shield her from the blast. The explosion painfully vibrated his eardrums and he could barely hear Samantha's muffled scream.

Little, solid pieces rained down on him and he became aware that the sky was raining zombie parts. The larger pieces began to fall and John was painfully struck in the back by an intact thigh. He winced but didn't move away from Samantha.

Just when he thought it was clear to lift his head, the sound of automatic gunfire sliced through the night.

The voices of screaming soldiers could be heard; the sounds of bombs going off in the background and the cries of the mortally wounded, knowing that death would come to take them away. People yelling in Iraqi, calling their praises to Allah. In his mind he saw the faces of dead women and children caught in the crossfire pitch forward and stare accusingly with blank eyes.

"John?" Samantha said and brought him back to reality.

"Just stay down. I'll try and get Kelly," he whispered and crawled off.

The shooting had stopped but there were now voices yelling in the distance. John stayed low and did his best to keep his face away from the ground, where pools of blood and flesh were already seeping into the moist dirt. Kelly was still draped over Mike, her head resting on his chest, her arms strewn across him.

"Kelly, let's go," John said quietly.

She ignored him.

"Damn it, Kelly, I'm sorry for your loss. Mike was a good friend and a great deputy and I'm gonna miss him, but I know he wouldn't want you to give up."

She wouldn't respond.

"Kelly, we need to go," he said and grabbed the back of her shirt and pulled.

Her head snapped back and rolled to the side, and that's when John saw the bullet that had hit her in the side of her head. He gently pushed her back so she could continue to embrace Mike.

"Goddamn it," he muttered and began to crawl back to Samantha. "Kelly's dead," he said as he watched her lips quiver and tears well up in her eyes.

"At least they went together," Samantha said.

"Yeah, that's kinda what I thought, too."

"Are we still going to make a run for it?"

"Yeah, but we have to stay low. The snipers are probably looking for movement."

"Wait, do you feel that?" she asked.

At first he didn't know what she meant, but a moment later he felt it too. Underneath him, he could feel the rumble of the ground intensify with each passing second.

He turned his head around and saw the approaching headlights of a patrol vehicle.

61

"Samantha," John whispered. "Stay down and don't do anything foolish." He sat up and raised his hands high in the air. "Hey! Don't shoot! We're not crazy!" he yelled while waving his hands back and forth.

The Army jeep screeched to a halt, the sound of M-16s being readied and aimed.

"Who said that? Show yourself, now!" the gruff voice of a soldier called out.

John looked over at Samantha. "Remember, just stay down and be quiet." She nodded and he slowly stood up, making sure his hands never moved and were in sight the entire time. He knew the odds were that these soldiers were nothing more than boys playing war, and with recent events, they all had itchy trigger fingers.

A stream of bright light coming from one of the spotlights mounted atop the jeep hit John square in the face and blinded him. He could make out the blurry shapes of four soldiers, all with guns drawn. He looked down and saw little red laser dots twitching slightly on his chest.

"Sir, you're trespassing in an area currently patrolled and secured by the United States Army. Any unauthorized movements will result in the use of lethal force. You will not be given a warning shot. Is this understood?" the gruff voice barked.

"Completely, sir," John said, not believing he'd just called some kid who was probably still in college 'sir.'

"Identify yourself."

"I'm Sheriff John Boudreaux of Cypress Pass, Louisiana. I'm a former Army Ranger."

"Are you alone? I heard you say *we* aren't crazy," the soldier said.

"I have one more with me. A woman, Samantha Worthing. She's also from Cypress Pass. She's normal, too."

"Tell her to show herself, slowly. No sudden movements!"

"It's okay, stand up," John said to her.

Samantha slowly rose off the ground and put her hands in the air. She was immediately blinded by the beam of light.

"Just you two?" the voice called.

"Yeah," John said. The 'sir' shit was over.

"We'll approach you. Don't move or resist us or you'll be shot. Understood?"

John nodded.

"Do you understand, Sheriff? Don't fuckin' nod your head at me. You answer me!"

"Yes!" John yelled.

The four soldiers hopped out of the jeep and cautiously approached John and Samantha. The first two reached Samantha first. They violently twisted her arms behind her back and handcuffed her. The other two soldiers grabbed John a second later and began to cuff him as well.

"Hey! What the fuck are you doing?" John yelled.

"It's procedure, sir," the soldier to his right said. "We're ensuring our safety while we transport you."

John turned to Samantha and saw one of the soldiers remove a piece of white cloth and douse it with liquid. He slapped it over Samantha's face. She issued a muffled cry and struggled to break free, but in seconds her eyes rolled up into the back of her head and she went limp.

"What the fuck are you doing?" John yelled and began to struggle.

The soldier prepared another piece of cloth and walked toward John, who kicked him in the stomach. The soldier crumpled to the ground.

John snapped his head to the side and smashed the soldier to his left in the face, just underneath his helmet. Just as he was about to break free and make a run for it, he was lifted off the ground as another soldier tackled him.

The air rushed out of his lungs and he landed hard, dirt getting into his mouth. He felt the wet cloth pressed over his nose and mouth, and before he could stop himself, he was breathing in the sweet smell of chloroform. His head begin to spin as his eyes got heavy.

"You bastards..." he slurred and slipped into unconsciousness.

62

Colonel Dillon sat behind his desk and pounded furiously on his keyboard as he filed a report. Project Revival was going to be hailed as a success and he was certain a large promotion would be his reward.

He wasn't pleased with the few 'escapees' during the project, but he felt the rough terrain would eliminate those few who had breached the containment. Still, there was no need to alert his superiors. He was almost finished with the daily email he sent to his contacts that summarized the day.

For a man of his high rank, his office was small and plain. The room was ten-by-ten square with a desk, phone and a computer. A small fern sat on the corner of his desk. The colonel believed it improved the room's air quality. A light knock at the door interrupted his train of thought. "Come in," he said as he continued typing.

"Sorry to disturb you, sir. We have survivors in custody."

"Excellent!" Dillon said. "Take me to them."

"Yes, sir, follow me, sir," the soldier said as Dillon stood up and followed.

63

When John came to, he was tied to a chair. His vision was blurry and his sides and head ached with pain.

Oh no, not again, he thought as he tried to lift his arms. The heavy leather straps held them down. He looked around and saw he was in what looked to be an interrogation room. A fluorescent light hung over his head and a large mirror was mounted on the wall next to him. He was facing a steel door.

He continued to struggle against the leather straps and noticed the chair was made of wood. He was debating slamming himself to the floor and seeing if that would break the chair, when a buzzer went off and the lock on the steel door slid open.

Colonel Dillon entered the room with another soldier.

"Leave us," Dillon said and the soldier promptly dismissed himself.

"Dillon..."John hissed, not at all surprised.

John attempted to see if he could somehow pull the leather straps away from the arms of the chair, but it was no use. As he tried to pull away, they only pulled back.

"Sheriff John Boudreaux," Dillon said with a large smile plastered across his face. "What a pleasant surprise this is, though I'm not at all shocked to see a Ranger sitting here before me."

"What the fuck is going on, Dillon? Why the fuck did I get cuffed and chloroformed?" John said, not amused by the strange welcome. "And where's Samantha?"

"All in good time, but for now I need you to relax. The soldiers are just following procedures. You know about procedures and orders yourself, I'm sure. You know you follow them without question."

"I'm tired of hearing about procedures. Where's Samantha?" he asked again. "And why am I tied up?"

"Don't worry, your girlfriend is in the next room being examined and questioned. And to answer your other question, you're tied up because you're viewed as a threat."

"A threat? How the fuck am I a threat?"

"I knew all about you, Sheriff, before I even set foot in your rancid little shit stain of a town. Your record is impressive to say the least. Excellent work in basic training, always placing first in individual drills. Your extensive time on the battlefield was commendable as well. You were captured and tortured horribly. Yet you survived and made it home. You're a model war hero."

"Yeah, I was a real war hero. That meant a lot to my wife when I got back. I lost everything because of my time over there."

"The life of a soldier is often a difficult one, Sheriff."

"What the hell does this have to do with me being tied up? What's going on around here?"

"Well, Sheriff, there were three of you that day when you were taken hostage. The other two were killed, you being the only survivor. That's not the only time you've been engaged in battle where everyone was killed and yet you were the only one to walk away. You're a lucky man, John. May I call you John?"

"So what, I got lucky," John replied, not answering the other question. He could care less what Dillon called him.

"Not necessarily just lucky, John. I'm seeing a pattern here, because now you're the only survivor of Cypress Pass." Dillon walked over to the mirror and flipped on the switch next to it.

The mirror was transparent glass, and John gasped at what was revealed on the other side.

64

Samantha was lying on her back, strapped to a metal surgical table, not moving. A tall cart with various saws, clamps, and scalpels stood next to the table. John couldn't see her face.

"What the fuck are you doing to her?" John demanded, not able to take his eyes off her.

"Be patient, soldier, you'll see," Dillon said, smiling like a jackal.

A pale man with frizzy white hair and dark-rimmed glasses walked into the room and stood over Samantha. John could have sworn he looked like Albert Einstein, and with all that had been going on, it wouldn't have surprised him if it was. The man was dressed in a white laboratory coat with a stethoscope draped around his neck. His coat did its best to hide the protruding gut that hung over his scrub pants.

He walked over to the cart and removed a syringe. Uncapping it, he plunged it into a vial containing a liquid that gave off a faint green aura. Once he'd drawn the proper amount, he placed the vial back on the cart.

"What's he doing to her?" John yelled, not looking away.

"She's just getting a little shot, John. That is Dr. Johannes Kreshnik. He's one of the most brilliant scientists in the world. He specializes in virology and pathology. We were fortunate the Swiss government loaned him to us to help with our little experiment."

"Experiment?" John asked, puzzled.

"Yes, John. You know full and well a weapon has to be tested several times before it's authorized for combat. It has to go through rigorous lab tests, then a thorough field test, and if it passes, it just might be ready for live combat."

"You can't possibly be saying what I think you're saying."

"There's a new era of warfare, John, the biological era. The United States has sat back and watched Third World shitholes develop diseases that would give you nightmares. If some ignorant camel farmers can do it, then goddamn it, we can do it better."

"I can't believe I'm hearing this."

"And why is that? Why are you so surprised? Would you be in favor of continuing to send our boys over there to die? Hell, you were over there, John. You know what it's like, what those people are like, and I use the term 'people' very loosely. They're animals. What if I told you that America could win a war without firing one bullet or losing one soldier? We drop our experiment over there, and simply let them kill each other. Then we come in and perform mop-up duty. The land, the oil, everything will be ours! It'll change the entire face of war. America will be unopposed."

"You let loose a biological weapon in an American city! Good people, hard working people, are dead! My friends are dead! And for what? For field testing? You're fucking crazy!"

Dillon walked over to John and knelt down so they were eye to eye. John's face grew hot with rage as Dillon's cold blue eyes pierced his.

"John, I'd hardly call Cypress Pass a city," he said with a laugh. "Isn't it great how easily Louisiana politicians can be bribed? You want to know what's really fucked up? The people you voted into office approved this. Now of course that dumbass mayor didn't truly know what was going on, but the higher ups did. All we had to do was put out a request for a small town with a controllable population to do some testing on, and Louisiana was the first state to volunteer. Cypress Pass was chosen at random. We practically drew it out of a hat." He laughed again.

John's head ached and begin to spin. Every word the colonel said came down on him like a hammer. He'd been doing his best to save his friends, but in the end it was impossible.

He was just a pawn in a war simulator. He gazed over at Samantha and saw the doctor was standing by her, patiently waiting.

"Tell Dr. Kreshnik to get on with it," Dillon ordered through a speaker system built into the wall.

A soldier walked into the room and said something to the doctor, who nodded his head and turned to look down on Samantha. He broke open a container of smelling salts and waved them under her nose. Her head began to shake almost immediately and her arms and legs began to fight the restraints.

Dillon placed a firm hand on John's shoulder, then bent down and whispered into his ear, "Just watch. It's quite fascinating really."

65

Ammonium carbonate filled Samantha's nostrils, burning her sinuses and waking her immediately. Upon trying to shield her eyes from the bright light overhead, she found her arms wouldn't move. Then she saw the man dressed in doctor's scrubs standing next to her.

Opening her mouth to call for help, the man brought a single finger to his mouth and motioned for her to shush. She was so confused that she did what he suggested. In his gloved hand he held a large syringe.

Her eyes went wide upon seeing it. "What's that for?" she asked, eyeing the needle with fright.

"It will make you feel better, my dear," he said in a heavy accent that Samantha couldn't place.

The doctor grabbed her arm and held onto it firmly. He was surprisingly strong and soon she felt the prickle of a needle thrust inside her vein. She cried out. Quickly the needle was removed and the pain subsided.

The doctor placed a hand on her head and mumbled a few words in his native tongue. It was a strange gesture and Samantha assumed it was meant to calm her down. He packed up his syringe and the vial and left the room, making sure to close the door behind him.

"John!" she called out, looking frantically around the room. Her eyes fell on the mirror but all she saw was her reflection.

The spot where the doctor injected her was already burning.

66

"You bastard! What did he inject her with? What is that stuff?" John yelled. Every vein in his forehead and neck became pronounced as he struggled to free himself.

"Now, now, John, try to stay calm. Just watch the transformation. It's truly an incredible process."

"No! Samantha!" John screamed at the soundproof glass. "So help me if I get free I'll kill you," John hissed through gritted teeth.

Dillon smiled. "Well, then I guess I shall have to make sure that doesn't happen, hmm?" He gestured to Samantha. "Now watch."

John could see her lying on the table. Her chest was rising and falling rapidly, too quickly to be normal.

67

At first, Samantha saw that the injection spot burned slightly and a small red bump began to rise up on her tan skin. Seconds later it felt like her arm was on fire. She could feel what she thought was liquid napalm coursing through her veins and reaching her heart.

She fell back on the table and gasped for air. With each breath she took, the next one became more difficult. Soon she was in full cardiac arrest and her breathing halted. The virus wrapped itself around her still heart and made a path to her brain.

Once there, it mingled with cells and neurons, turning the recently dead synapses back on. The resurrection was almost complete.

68

"Samantha?" John whispered as tears began to blur his vision.

Her chest was no longer rising. Her limbs were still and her head was awkwardly tilted to the side. John managed to choke down a sob. He pushed the cry back down inside his stomach and added it to the deposit of rage, anger, and hate that was quickly consuming him. He turned to Dillon who still had a smile on his face.

"You bastard! You sick fucking bastard! How can you do this to people, to innocent people you're supposed to be protecting?"

"It's for the greater good, John, now please, try to calm down," Dillon said nonchalantly.

John began struggling against the straps that bound him when a loud beep sounded. Dillon walked over to the door, pressed a button and Dr. Kreshnik strode in.

"Hello, Doctor," Dillon said. "Good work, as usual."

"Thank you, Colonel," Kreshnik replied.

Kreshnik opened his medicine bag and removed a fresh syringe and a vial of the deadly liquid. There was a biohazard label across it and some words John didn't understand; whether they were Swedish or organic chemistry was irrelevant in the end.

"Ah, here we are," Dillon said with a smile as Kreshnik filled the syringe.

Dillon and Kreshnik turned to face John and the doctor began slowly walking toward him.

"No!" John yelled as he fought the leather straps. "Keep that bastard away from me!"

"John, just relax. It doesn't even hurt. Well, I assume it doesn't hurt, not like any of the others had much to say after it took effect."

The sound of Kreshnik and Dillon laughing at the crude joke sent a chill down his spine.

He continued to fight against the straps but his muscles were starting to grow tired and ache with each pull. Kreshnik began to lean in and John knew his time was running out.

Then one last idea popped in his head and he acted on it instantly.

Kreshnik was less than three feet away when John planted his left leg hard into the floor and pushed himself back. Swinging his right foot out, he caught Kreshnik just underneath the chin.

The doctor let out a howl of shock and pain and fell backwards, the syringe sailing through the air to land on the floor five feet away.

John collided with the floor hard, and when he did, the old wooden chair splintered and broke apart. As soon as he knew his freedom was obtained, he rolled backwards and settled in a crouch position. The entire display of acrobatics took only a few seconds, and Dillon was stunned to see John staring at him with an intensity that rivaled the monsters he'd been responsible for creating.

John sprung forward like a cat pouncing toward a bird, and in that moment Dillon wished he'd been armed with his pistol, which was on his desk in his office.

As John's shoulder drove into the colonel's gut, the air left Dillon's lungs. Realizing immediately that he had the upper hand, John pummeled Dillon with punishing blows to the head and chest, the leather straps swinging from his wrists to also strike Dillon.

The colonel collapsed onto the floor, unable to defend himself against his bigger and faster opponent.

Then John spotted the syringe a few feet away. He rolled off Dillon, driving his knee hard into the battered colonel's stomach as he did, and picked the syringe up off the floor. Just as he was preparing to turn around, he felt a hand grab his ankle.

He looked down and saw Kreshnik gasping for air through his shattered jaw. The doctor was trying to talk but couldn't form the words as blood poured onto the floor out of his mouth. John wasn't in the mood for listening anyway.

With a mighty stomp, he crushed Kreshnik's throat. The doctor convulsed for a few seconds and then went still.

When John looked at the two-way mirror, Samantha caught his eye.

She was no longer lying motionless on the metal table but was now thrashing about. Her head rolled to the side and John's heart dropped when he saw her face.

Her eyes were cloudy white, her mouth a sneer, a thin string of drool escaping through the corner of her lips. Her teeth snapped the air and her limbs flailed wildly against the restraints that she didn't understand. Her gaze seemed to lock right onto John, and in her eyes, he could see anger and pain.

"You son-of-a-bitch," John said and walked over to Dillon, who was attempting to crawl out of the room.

He stood over the colonel who was making every effort to reach the speaker system on the wall. Dillon was given a hard knee to the back for his efforts. John wrapped a muscular forearm around Dillon's neck and forced the man to his feet. He could feel the colonel wobble as he stood upright. Blood from Dillon's busted nose and lips flowed onto John's forearm. John brought the needle up to Dillon's eye.

"Start walking to the door," John growled through clenched teeth.

"John, don't do this. Just listen to me," Dillon pleaded.

"Shut the fuck up!" John screamed, so loud that Dillon's right ear began to ring with tinnitus.

Dillon stumbled forward to the speaker system. He began to place his hand to the button to make a call when he stopped. "John, you won't get out of here. This unit is one of the best we have. There's more than just weekend warriors here!"

John replied by ramming the sharp needle through Dillon's left shoulder. Dillon howled in pain as John clamped his hand over the man's mouth. Dillon's hot breath hit the back of his hand with each gasp the man made.

"Shut up and do what I say, or so help me I'll inject you and kill you, wait for you to turn, and then fucking kill you again." He pressed Dillon's face against the speaker. "Make them open it, and you better sound normal."

Dillon took a deep breath and slowly clear his throat. He reached up with his right hand and pressed the button. "Open the door. I'm ready to leave," Dillon said in a voice with no emotion.

It was so clear and so effortless that it made John uneasy. How could someone who had just received a thorough ass kicking and have a needle sticking in their shoulder that could turn them into a walking corpse be so calm? The door beeped open, and as soon as it did, Dillon tried to escape.

"Kill him! It's a trap!" Dillon yelled as he tried to tear away from John's grasp.

"Bastard!" John screamed as he grabbed Dillon.

Colonel Jacob Dillon was a fine soldier; one of the toughest men around, but even he wasn't prepared for the whirlwind of rage that was John Boudreaux. With the quickness of a cat, John spun Dillon toward him. He delivered a devastating knee to Dillon's side, which would have caused him to drop to the floor if John wasn't holding him up.

He pulled Dillon upright by the shirt collar and gave him a kick to the spine which sent him sprawling. Just before John landed the kick, he pushed the syringe down, releasing the virus into Dillon.

The colonel slid on the floor briefly before coming to a stop.

A soldier came rushing into the room, brandishing an impact baton which he swung wildly. John caught the young soldier's arm in mid-strike and flipped him over. As the soldier hit the floor, John was already behind him.

With a quick turn of his arms, the soldier's neck snapped easily and the body went limp. John stood up and grabbed the baton and the 9mm in the soldier's hip holster.

Dillon was staring at John with eyes that looked like they were on fire. He was holding his neck and appeared to be choking. His face was beet red and veins stretched across his face and throat.

"You don't want to miss this, Dillon. It's really quite fascinating," John hissed as the colonel began to seizure.

69

John exited the room and was greeted by a corridor of white walls and multiple doors. It reminded him of a hospital, but he knew the closest hospital was miles away. He paused for a few seconds until he was sure no one was coming. The young soldier he'd killed had probably been so nervous that he didn't think to call for help. John hoped that was the case and didn't feel any sympathy for killing him.

Before he found his way out, he knew there was one thing he had to do. When he came to the first door on his left, he turned the handle and opened it. Before him, flailed Samantha.

The sound that passed through her lips was horrible. It was of death clawing at a window. Of a soul damned for all eternity. The sound of a person trapped in misery. John stood at the end of the metal table and lightly touched her foot. It was cool and clammy against his skin. He could feel the tears starting to well up. She went wild at the sensation of his touch and began snapping her teeth ferociously at him. White, frothy spittle flew in the air as she whipped her head from side to side, trying her best to get him.

"I'm so sorry I let you down, Samantha. I said I'd save you, but in the end I failed. I failed everyone. I'm so sorry." The tears flowed freely. "You made me feel good about myself for the first time in years. You made me care about someone other than myself. I'll never forget you for that. I only wish I'd had the courage to have gotten to know you sooner."

Samantha continued to howl and thrash.

"I promised you that I'd never let you be one of them. And I won't let you be one any longer."

He looked down and saw a small white medical pillow on the floor. He picked it up and walked over to her. Her teeth eagerly snapped the air with anticipation of him getting closer. Spittle flew from her snarling mouth.

John placed the pillow firmly on her face, her teeth taking hold and biting into the soft material. He pushed down so her head was flat on the bed and raised the gun taken from the young soldier. He pressed it firmly to the pillow where her forehead was.

"I'm so sorry," he whispered and squeezed the trigger. A soft pop filled the room as the pillow absorbed most of the noise. Samantha's head jerked back, the white pillow already turning a crimson red. He heard her issue one final moan and then she went still, to never move again.

John paused for only a brief moment so the emotion could pass. It passed surprisingly quickly. He'd just killed someone he really cared for, but he was in full soldier mode now. Emotions didn't have a place when one was in this mindset.

He fled into the dimly lit hallway again and cautiously walked down the narrow corridor. As he passed the many closed doors, he couldn't help but wonder what horrors possibly lay behind them.

He'd extended Samantha a form of mercy and thought maybe he should consider doing the same for any other unfortunates who had fallen into Colonel Dillon's monstrous plan.

But in the end, reason gave way and he decided it would be a better plan to get out while he still could. As John reached the end of the hallway, he was greeted by a small, metal sign that simply read **BARRACKS** and had an arrow pointing to the right.

He turned the corner and walked down the short hall until he reached the door at the very end.

On the door was a metal sign with the word: **EXIT**.

He cracked the door open slightly and was greeted by a rush of warm air. Peering out of the small opening, he gazed into the barracks tent. Rows of bunk beds lined the sides of the tent for fifty feet.

A row of lights were strung across the center of the ceiling, lighting up the middle but casting shadows around the beds. He didn't see any activity inside so he entered.

John immediately went to the left side and hugged the wall, making sure the shadows hid him from any possible patrols. As he quietly made his way to the front of the tent, he spotted a single guard sitting on a crate, smoking a cigarette. John started to twitch in anticipation of a puff of nicotine.

He crept toward the unsuspecting guard, and just as the soldier raised his hand for another drag, John brought the baton crashing into the man's temple.

With his left arm, he nestled the soldier's head and swiftly pulled him inside the tent.

He dragged the man to one of the beds closest to the entrance and began searching him.

Two clips were found for his pistol and the soldier's identification badge, complete with some kind of magnetic scanning device. John's heart fluttered when he found a thin box in the man's pocket—a pack of cigarettes.

But as he opened the pack, his spirits fell when he saw the emptiness of the container staring back at him.

"Damn it," he muttered, then crumpled the pack and threw it on the floor, where it rolled under a bed.

He looked at the soldier and knew the man was dead. The baton had caved in the side of his head, most likely killing him before he even knew what had happened.

Blood still leaked slowly from the wound.

As John pulled a sheet over the soldier, he hoped his escape would remain a quiet one.

70

Colonel Dillon was doing all he could do to hold on for a few more seconds. He could feel the searing fire coursing through his veins and his muscles kept spasming in rapid succession.

His vision was starting to blur, and he knew he had only moments before the virus took hold for good. He crawled on his hands and knees toward the buzzer on the wall intercom.

As he crawled forward, he left a trail of greenish foam which was pouring from his mouth. He couldn't help but think of all the people he'd willingly transformed in the past few weeks, how many of them had cursed his name.

Was this a proper revenge for them? That he would suffer a similar fate? They would never understand the sacrifices that had to be made to ensure the prosperity of their country. Colonel Dillon was simply a soldier to the core, an old school soldier who was given an order and didn't question it.

It wasn't his place to challenge the people who ran the country. Right now, he was going to make sure that a certain former Ranger didn't escape and ruin the valuable weapon that was in its final stages of testing.

With a scream that could have frozen water, Dillon lurched to his feet and stumbled forward. He smacked the wall hard and his hand flailed out and jammed the button for the alarm.

Suddenly, the welcoming sound of a siren wailing filled his ears. It was like music, a beautiful symphony.

Dillon collapsed to the floor and his last living thought was that he was a damn fine soldier.

He closed his eyes and his heart stopped; the transformation was almost complete.

71

The wail of the siren told John his escape was about to become a lot more difficult. A red light overhead began circling and cast a burgundy glow inside the dim barracks. The shout of soldiers outside the tent came to him; some barking orders, others asking questions, and more in general confusion.

He loaded the pistol with a fresh clip and poked his head out of the tent, trying frantically to plan his next move. A firefight was the last thing he wanted. Outside, he saw soldiers running back and forth. They were all traveling to their stations and most had their backs turned to the tent. John saw a long white building nestled next to the barracks tent. When the coast was clear, he ran for it, making sure to stay hidden in the shadows.

He grabbed the metal handle of the door and pulled it open. Once inside, he found himself facing another hallway. At the end of the corridor was a pair of double metal doors. He made his way forward with his gun drawn. When he opened the doors, he found himself in a laboratory. Rows of beakers and tubes, some empty, others bubbling with strange concoctions, lined the tables. A scientist, a thin frail looking man with gray hair and glasses, looked up at him, startled.

"Can I help you?" he asked in a thick European accent.

"No, just continue your work," John said, trying to act like he belonged. He made his way though the room to a second pair of doors, one half open. Just as he reached the doorway, he saw three helmet-clad heads run past it. John ducked down quickly. He waited a few moments and then checked again to make sure the area was clear.

"What are you doing in here?" the scientist asked, but John ignored him.

With his finger on the trigger, John slowly walked though the doorway and into yet another hallway. It was empty, so he proceeded down the corridor with caution. As he came to the end of the hallway, he was presented with an option to go left or right. As he peered around the right corner, one of the soldiers spotted him.

"Halt!" he heard the soldier bark as John ducked back behind the corner. He could hear footsteps running toward him. John took a deep breath and visualized the soldiers running. He spun around the corner and fired, taking the first soldier down instantly. The other two soldiers jumped to the side rooms. The soldier on the left was lucky, his door was open. The soldier on the right was not. As he raised his leg to kick the door down, John sent a bullet into his skull.

Two down, one to go, he thought as he felt a bullet whiz by his head.

The last soldier was hanging out of the door entrance and firing wildly. John whipped around and fired a few rounds at him. He tried aiming for the doorframe to see if the bullet would go through, but luck wasn't on his side and the soldier continued to fire.

John knew his time was running out. If he didn't act soon, it would only be a matter of time before more soldiers arrived, drawn to the sound of gunshots.

When reinforcements arrived, and they would arrive eventually, he would be royally screwed.

"Ugh!" John cried as he collapsed to the floor and tossed his gun to the side, sliding it into the hallway.

He could hear the soldier's footsteps drawing closer and for a brief moment felt sorry for the poor kid, as he walk into the trap John had just laid.

John gripped the baton and waited. As the soldier reached the corner, John spun around and brought the baton forward into the soldier's throat. The kid gasped as he grabbed his crushed throat and dropped to the floor, spitting blood. Within seconds he was motionless.

After retrieving his gun, he released the clip and removed a fresh one from the soldier's belt.

He loaded his weapon and ran down the hall. As he dashed around another corner, he collided hard into a woman.

The collision caused him to stumble backwards but sent the unsuspecting woman sliding across the floor. John quickly composed himself and drew his gun.

"Who the hell are you?" he growled.

The woman was no more than a kid fresh out of college. She was probably in her mid-twenties, with a thin frame and black hair. Her glasses gave her an attractive, nerdy quality, and she had a row of freckles splashed across her nose.

She had on a red shirt and black pants. An identification tag hung around her neck. She was trying to find her voice, but her eyes were wide at the sight of the gun pointed at her.

"I'll repeat it one more time. Who the fuck are you?" John demanded.

The woman began stuttering. She was breathing heavily and tears were in her eyes. He didn't want her to break down into a full panic. He checked down both hallways and holstered his gun, then knelt down beside her.

"Look, I'm sorry for scaring you. I won't hurt you, I promise, but I need your help. Help me find a car or truck that I can use to get out of here."

She began to cry. "I...I don't know," she sobbed and placed her hands over her face.

"What do you mean 'you don't know'? How did you get here?"

She took a few seconds to compose herself before answering. "They bussed us here."

"Who are they?"

"The Army, the military, I don't know."

"So if you aren't in the Army, then what're you doing here?"

"I'm an I T specialist. They said they needed me to work on a new program."

John helped her to her feet and wrapped his hand around her thin wrist. He drew his gun. "You're coming with me."

"But I don't know anything. Please, let me go," she pleaded.

"I said you're coming with me, and for your sake, don't do anything stupid," he warned and raised the pistol.

She nodded her head in understanding.

"What's your name?"

"Cindy."

"Hi, Cindy. I'm John. Just help me get out of here and everything'll be okay."

"You promise?"

"I promise I'll let you go as soon as I'm away from here."

She nodded her head again and John let go of her wrist.

"Where do they keep the buses?"

"I don't know."

He grabbed her around the neck and slammed her hard into the wall, then pressed the muzzle of the gun into her forehead.

"Don't fuck with me, Cindy! You better start remembering!" he hissed through clenched teeth.

"I don't know," she choked. "They pick me up and drop me off every day."

She closed her eyes and began to cry hot tears. "I'm not lying. I promise."

"Freeze!" snapped a voice from down the hall.

"Shit!" John hissed. Four soldiers were heading toward him with guns drawn.

John kicked open the first door he saw and pulled Cindy into the room with him. They entered into a surprisingly plush office, but John didn't have time to admire it.

There was a wooden desk in front of them and he dove behind it, dragging Cindy with him. He pushed the desk over onto its side and was happy that it was difficult to do so. Real wood would stop a bullet better than cheap particle board.

He took a ready stance behind the desk; his pistol was steady, as were his eyes on the doorway. Cindy was in a fetal position next to him.

A soldier burst through the doorway and John cut him down quickly with two bullets to the chest.

The soldier stumbled backwards and hit the wall behind him, then slid down to the floor, leaving a bloody streak on the wall in his wake. Another soldier's hand appeared in the doorway.

The gun flailed wildly about as the soldier blindly fired inside the office. Cindy began to crawl out from behind the desk.

"Jesus, what the fuck are you doing?" John yelled and pushed her back down. "Keep your head down before you lose it!"

The firing from the soldier stopped and John returned fire. He aimed at the doorway and walls near it, hoping a bullet would find its way through the plaster to the other side. The same hand reappeared and the firing resumed.

John ducked down low behind the desk and took cover. The bullets flew like hornets, and holes appeared in the walls, objects shattering.

He looked up and saw a large window above them. Taking aim, he fired three shots into the window, causing the glass to shatter. Rechecking his clip, he saw it was empty, so he loaded the gun with his final clip and waited.

72

"Colonel Dillon? Sir, are you all right?" a soldier asked as he approached the colonel, who was slumped against the wall.

The soldier touched Dillon's shoulder and immediately knew something wasn't right. The colonel's shoulder was stiff; there was no reaction to the touch. Then, Dillon's head snapped up and his cloudy eyes locked onto the soldier's throat.

"Colonel? What are you..." the soldier began as Dillon clamped his teeth around the soft throat.

Dillon took the young soldier to the floor and began to feed. For more than a minute he feasted on the warm flesh. Then he heard other voices and lost interest in his food. Standing awkwardly, he stumbled out the doorway, into the hallway, and toward the noise source. A few minutes later, the soldier lying on the floor joined him.

73

The soldier's blind fire had ceased and John used the momentary quiet to inform Cindy of his latest plan. "When I get up to shoot, jump out the window."

"No! They want you, not me! You jump out and leave me here!"

"If you don't go I'll shoot you right now and I'll leave."

She gasped at his threat and began to slowly move toward the window, careful not to crawl on any broken glass. John didn't have time to wait. He rose to his feet with his gun aimed at the empty doorway. With his left arm, he lifted her off the floor and pushed her up to the window. Just then a soldier entered the room and John shot him. Other soldiers were yelling as they came from down the hall, and in seconds John knew he'd be trapped. With a push, he sent Cindy flying out the window and into the dark night. He fired two more shots at the doorway to keep any adventurous souls from trying anything, turned, and jumped out the window behind her.

As he hit the ground, he tucked his legs in and rolled to a soft stop. Cindy wasn't aware of this trick and took the force of the six foot fall with her back, causing the air to rush out of her lungs. He rushed over to her and helped her up.

With him not shooting at the soldiers, they only had seconds before the soldiers would be brave enough to enter the room. As

John turned the corner of the building, he spotted a small diesel tank with a soldier fueling a jeep.

John placed Cindy, who was still gasping for air, on the ground behind a stack of crates as he crept up to the unsuspecting man. He withdrew the baton and placed it behind his back.

"Hey, pal, you got the time?" John asked casually, his face lost in shadows.

"Uh yeah," the soldier said, startled.

The soldier peered down at his watch. "It's..."

Before he could tell John that the time was almost 0700 hours, John struck the man in the throat.

He collapsed to the ground, gripping his neck and struggling to breathe. John rushed back to where Cindy was and helped her up. They made their way back to the gray, Army-issue jeep and he helped her in the passenger side.

Then he ran around and jumped behind the steering wheel. The key was in the ignition and the engine started right up. He stepped on the gas and pulled forward, making sure not to go fast enough to draw suspicion.

74

"Are you all right?" John asked Cindy, who was pressed against the seat, cowering in fear.

"I'm fine," she muttered.

"Where should I go, Cindy? You have to know something."

"Take a right at the road up ahead. There's a checkpoint. It'll take you to the highway."

There was silence as John made the turn.

"Where are you taking me?" she asked.

"Just keep quiet and stay cool. As soon as I'm on that highway, you're free to go."

He could see the checkpoint ahead as he continued driving. It was only a single guard shack with a gate arm on each side. For a moment, he debated just shooting the guard, but then decided to just play this one by the book. He could always shoot the guard if things took a turn for the worse.

"You're not going to get through. The alarm's sounded. Only military personnel can leave."

John dug in his pocket and removed an ID and magnetic card from the first soldier he'd killed. He brought the jeep to a slow stop and flashed the magnetic card in front of the scanner. The guard looked up casually, not seeing a threat. The red light on the machine turned green. The soldier in the guard shack walked over to the open window.

"Where ya headed?" he asked.

"Certified courier for Colonel Dillon. I'm instructed to remove this civilian from the camp immediately for security reasons," John said smoothly as he held up the dead soldier's ID.

The guard looked inside the jeep at Cindy who was still huddled against the seat. She stared straight forward and didn't make eye contact. John reached over and unclipped her ID and handed it to the guard.

"She's scared. I have to get her out of here," John said calmly.

"Sure thing. Hey, what's going on in there? They don't tell us guys on watch nothing."

"One of the colonel's experiments escaped."

"No shit, huh?"

"Yeah. Better keep an eye out. If you find it, I bet you'd get a promotion."

"Thanks, I'll do that," the guard smiled. He walked into the shack and the metal arm began to rise. "Go ahead."

John gave a slight wave as he drove onward to freedom.

75

The highway was pitch dark and free of cars, but John didn't notice nor would he have cared. He was doing his best to come down from the adrenaline high that had been surging through his body, his mind racing with ideas of where he should go next.

"I thought you were going to let me out?" Cindy asked.

"I know a place..." John said, trailing off.

"You know a place, what?" Cindy said, puzzled.

"A place. A good place to go. Usually has a lot of cops."

She let out a sigh and stared out the window into the dark forest that was zipping by her.

"Good, I hope they arrest you when we get there."

John slammed on the brakes and the jeep squealed to a stop in the middle of the road.

"What are you doing?" Cindy demanded.

"Do you have any idea what those people were doing back there?" John screamed. His face was blood red. Spittle flew from his mouth and landed on Cindy's glasses. She sat back against her seat, fear suddenly washing over her.

"Or what you were helping them do?" he screamed while pointing an accusing finger in her face.

"We...we were testing the water," Cindy said, her voice low.

"Water? What the fuck for?"

"Ph levels and possible biological microorganisms. Like coliforms. Bio-diesel products and pesticides as well. They wanted me to manage the data input and setup spreadsheets and other programs for data tracking."

He stared forward. Cindy was starting to get even more scared, and when John lowered his head to the steering wheel and started laughing, she almost jumped out and ran into the night.

"It was the water," he said and began to giggle. The laugh formed inside his stomach and suddenly erupted out of his throat like a volcano. "The fucking water!" he exclaimed and slapped the steering wheel.

"You're scaring me. What're you talking about?"

"They poisoned the water."

"Who? You aren't making any sense."

"The fucking Army. They were putting something—that virus—in the water system."

"A virus? What virus? Why would our military do that?"

He didn't answer her; instead he removed his foot from the brake pedal and continued driving.

"Do you have any cigarettes?" he asked.

"I don't smoke," she said coldly. "Are you going to tell me what you're talking about?"

"Dillon told me they were testing a new biological weapon. My town got chosen to be the lucky guinea pig in this big experiment. They must have contaminated the water. That explains why everyone changed so fast. It all makes sense now."

"Changed? Who changed?"

"The whole city. Cypress Pass. I had to watch one of the only people I've ever cared about get injected with that shit."

"Okay, I'm still not following."

He began fumbling for cigarettes. He checked the glove box, the center console, and the side of the doors. Nothing.

"The Army, our United States Army, poisoned the water supply of my town to test a new weapon. The entire town has turned into a bunch of walking, cannibalistic corpses. They were dead, but at the same time they were alive. It was almost like they were a shell of their former selves. Just walking around looking for a meal."

"Are you serious? That's ridiculous. Dead people don't walk around. It's a medical impossibility," Cindy said.

John ignored her. He was starting to regret not dumping her in the highway the moment he'd escaped the camp, but soon he saw the lights of the diner in the distance and he forgot all about it.

"It's right up here," he said.

76

John pulled the jeep into the parking lot of Winston's Diner and parked it between two police cars. Two more police units were parked to the side.

"All right, just stay put. I'm going inside to tell them what's been happening."

Cindy nodded her head and gave him a small smile. He returned it with one of his own.

He walked up the concrete slope to the door and entered the diner. A metal bell above the door announced his arrival. The smell of greasy fries and cleaning solution filled his nostrils. The diner was mostly full, some beefy truck drivers having stopped for an early breakfast. John spotted a table of four police officers and slowly walked toward them.

"Excuse me, officers," he said.

The officers looked up from their meal and stared at John. They were tired and showed the wear and tear that came with working the night shift. However, they all did a double take at the bloody, bruised, and filthy mess that was standing in front of them.

"My name's Sheriff John Boudreaux. I'm from..."

The bell above the diner door clanged violently and everyone's attention was drawn to Cindy as she ran into the diner. "He kidnapped me!" she yelled and pointed at John. "He threatened to kill me!"

John quickly turned his attention back to the officers who were all trying to get up as fast as they could. John ran toward Cindy and removed his pistol from the back of his pants. He wrapped his forearm around her neck and pressed the gun hard into her temple.

All four of the officers drew their guns and leveled them at John and Cindy. One of the officers dropped back and John saw him raise his two-way radio to his mouth, calling in the situation.

The first cop who stood up was a tall, slightly pudgy officer with a bald head and a thick brown mustache. He looked into John's eyes and spoke in a clear, firm voice.

"Sir, put the gun down. Whatever the problem is, it's not worth it."

John snickered lightly. "You have no idea about my problems or the problem you're about to be dealing with."

"He's crazy! Help me!" Cindy whimpered, sobbing uncontrollably as John pressed his arm tighter against her throat.

"Come on, man, we can talk about this. Just put the gun down," the officer said again.

"I'm not putting my fucking gun down! You don't understand what they are! How they act! What they want! They destroyed my town!"

"Who?"

"The dead. They're walking. They'll eat you! You'll become one of them!"

John screamed, spittle flying from his mouth. Why wouldn't they listen? What was wrong with them?

One of the other officers began walking forward and John aimed the gun at him.

"Get the fuck back, man!" John ordered.

The bell above the door rang again, and as John turned slightly to see who was behind him, Cindy took advantage of his distraction to lunge away from him, escaping his grip. He knew it was too late even as she fell to the floor. *Damn rookie mistake*, he thought and heard the loud bang of a gun sound from behind him. Multiple bullets shredded his back and legs.

His gun fell from his hands and Cindy crawled across the floor of the diner. John dropped to the floor and stared up at the ceiling. A second later, a cop was standing over him holding a smoking shotgun, the barrel aimed at his chest.

Blood pooled around John as he lay on the floor. He suddenly felt very cold and his mouth was devoid of all moisture. The other four officers rushed around him and one kicked his gun out of the way.

"They're coming..." John muttered through gasping breaths. Blood began to seep out of his mouth and he began to choke. "Just...shoot 'em...in...the...head," he gasped as a blood bubble popped upon escaping his lips. He knew the end was near. His eyes were locked on the wooden ceiling fan gently spinning on its rod above him.

The blades began to turn and change with each passing rotation. He saw Mike and Kelly smiling at him; Mike with his classic goofy grin. Simone was standing next to them with a platter of biscuits and a hot thermos of coffee. The fan blades spun faster and faster. Samantha joined them and waved at him. Her eyes sparkled like diamonds, not like the muddled white pools he'd seen earlier before he'd killed her.

He blinked and they were gone.

The lights around him were starting to go dim. Just before the lights went out, he saw his daughter, Jenny, riding by on her little pink tricycle. Her blonde curls were bouncing in the air as she laughed and giggled.

"I'll miss you, Daddy," she said, laughing merrily as she drove by.

John took one last gasp of air, and was still.

77

"Who's coming?" one of the officers asked. "What the hell was he talking about?"

The first officer shrugged. "Who knows? Guy was crazy, on drugs maybe."

"If not drugs then maybe he cracked, went nuts, wouldn't be the first time," the officer with the shotgun said.

"Well, better get the coroner on the way so they can haul his dead ass out of here," the cop with the mustache said. "Let's see if you got any ID on you?" the cop said to John's corpse as he bent down and felt though his pockets. His hand found a wallet and he opened it. Staring at him was the badge of the Cypress Pass Sheriff and identification of John Boudreaux.

"Holy shit, this guy is a sheriff," the mustached cop muttered. His mind was already starting to race with all the problems this was going to cause him.

"Hey, hon, can I get a coffee to go?" the officer with the shotgun asked the waitress, who was still staring in shock at the corpse on her diner floor. All the patrons were silent, most having just risen from the floor, where they'd fallen in fear of being shot by a stray bullet. Slowly, the murmuring began as everyone began talking about the scene that had played out moments ago.

The officers didn't know what was coming their way. The truckers that were quietly eating their chicken fried steak and eggs didn't know either. They'd wanted to leave, but the officers made them stay for eye witness testimony. The cook flipping omelets behind the counter didn't know, and neither did the elderly waitress serving coffee.

No one had a clue that a wave of walking dead was heading their way. The undead, like a plague of locust, were slowly traveling up the highway. They shambled and moaned, their stiff legs dragging across the asphalt.

Everlasting and unquenchable hunger consumed their dull minds. Their only thought—if it could be considered a thought—was to feed that urge.

"Do you hear something?" Cindy asked the officer with the shotgun as he helped her to a table. "It sounds like people moaning."

"Probably just the wind," the officer replied as he left her and began organizing the patrons of the diner to take each report. "I'm sure it's nothing."

AFTERWORD

A few years ago, after watching yet another horrible zombie movie, a thought popped into my head. *I can do better*, I thought as I cringed at the awful dialogue and the cheap (but not awesome cheap) special effects. A story came to my mind and I immediately began writing. This was the moment I started my love affair with zombie literature.

As of late, zombies have become a bit of a punch line. They seem to be injected with humor because in actuality, they are simply terrifying. They're the king of the monsters. Vampires are romantic; werewolves can return back to their human form, and mummies…well, mummies are dried husks wrapped in gauze.

Zombies, however, are simply that: zombies. Slow moving, un-relenting, always on the search for human flesh. What makes them so horrifying is the psychological toll they take on the human mind. It is the idea that your mom, your dad, your children, or maybe even your best friend will look at you with nothing but hunger. The person you know will be standing before you, but inside is a primal brain acting on one urge: to feed. Nothing you say or do will bring that person back, and that right there is the greatest mind-fuck of all! How do you bring yourself to kill the person you loved unconditionally? Can you do it? Or do you join them? This is the reason why zombies are king.

This book, which you are holding, is an homage to George Romero's classic zombies. Over the years he has tinkered with his creation a bit by giving zombies the ability to learn or to adapt. In my zombie universe, however, this doesn't happen. There is no learning how to use tools. No communicating with the living. No remorse. No emotions. No mercy.

I'm taking it back to the beginning. Back to a time where the hero isn't a comedian killing thousands of zombies in a variety of whacky ways. No slapstick comedy here (and I absolutely loved Shaun of the Dead). This is pure horror. This is survival. There are no jokes.

The person I would like to thank the most for this book is my cousin, Paul. For starters it is because of him that I have my love for zombies and for all horror in general. While taking a screenplay course in college, he wrote a simple screenplay that was a little over a hundred pages long. It was not well received by his teacher and it sort of fell by the way side; unfairly tossed away as a waste of time. I asked him for a copy of it to read one day and what I read excited me. It was a simple, yet very solid story. I asked him for permission to turn it into a novel and he said yes. It was fun adding to the crude outline and turning it into something so much more. With this literary skeleton, I was able to add the organs, muscles, and flesh. I hope I've made him proud in bringing his screenplay to life.

To you, the reader, I thank you for dedicating your time to reading this book. You're the reason I write. The thought of sharing my story fills me with excitement and gives me the motivation to keep writing. To all the old-school zombie fans, I hope this satisfies and exceeds your zombie expectations. To all the new-school zombie fans, I hope you find a thrill in the slow-moving world of the undead. I will continue to write and do my best to contribute to this wonderful genre. I hope you will stay with me for the ride!

Mark Christopher

Made in the USA
Monee, IL
10 June 2026

53029978R00115